W9-BSH-661

MY ONLY SUNSHINE

for Donald

My Only Sunshine

a novel by
Lou Dischler

HUB CITY PRESS
SPARTANBURG, SC
2010

Copyright © 2010
Hub City Press

All rights reserved. No part of this
book may be reproduced in any form
or by any electronic or mechanical
means, including information storage
and retrieval systems, without
permission in writing from the
publisher, except by a reviewer, who
may quote brief passages in a review.

First printing, October 2010

Book design: Emily Louise Smith
Proofreaders: Peter Caster, Jan Scalisi,
and Betsy Teter
Printed in China by Everbest through
Four Colour Imports, Louisville, KY
Cover photograph © Hulton-Deutsch
Collection / Corbis

Library of Congress
Cataloging-in-Publication Data

Dischler, Lou, 1951–
My Only Sunshine / Lou Dischler.
p. cm.
ISBN 978-1-891885-72-3
1. Families—Fiction.
2. Louisiana—Fiction.
I. Title.
PS3604.I83M9 2010
813'.6—dc22
2010009074

186 W. Main Street
Spartanburg, SC 29306
864.577.9349 · www.hubcity.org

THE TOWN IN THIS STORY no longer exists; it drowned some years ago. But in 1962, Red Church was a bustling mill town known locally as "America's Sweet Tooth," as it refined sugar for the vast sugarcane plantations of the Louisiana lowcountry. This was an idyllic time and place for a boy like Charlie Boone, especially as Charlie was unaware that Russians were building missile bases in Cuba to lob hydrogen bombs over his head. He was also unaware that his notorious uncle had escaped from prison and was just a few miles up the road. No, on this lazy Saturday afternoon, Charlie's only concern was a wingless variety of thumb-sized wasps he thought were ants.

DAYS OF SUGAR

1

With all the hurricanes breezing in from the gulf, farmhouses were set off the ground on stilts. Kids could run under them standing up, which we did, barefoot in the cool dust. We didn't run up the steps to the house, though, because red velvet ants hung out there, and if one bit your foot it could swell up and burst open. That happened to a boy over in New Iberia. My teacher said he was lucky just to lose his toes, and we were all pretty impressed.

I was thinking of that because my brother was stuck on the steps, hollering. I was sure he'd been stung by a velvet the way he was carrying on, but no, it was just a couple of tree ants on his leg. I brushed them off. He'd dropped his Mason jar and it had rolled down. Root beer was foaming over the gray-painted wood, and he was still carrying on.

"It hurts!"

"What hurts?"

"My feet!"

"Well move, you dope. This wood's hot."

I had to push him down the steps 'cause he was prone to freezing up. "I don't get it," my grandfather had said. "Least thing, he freezes up."

"Stop freezing up," I said now. "If something hurts you, get away from it."

He said okay like he understood, but I knew he didn't. I handed him his jar, then raced him over to the pecan grove and beat him by a mile. He was bowlegged, so I wasn't going to brag about it, but I did like to win. He began picking up pecans and dropping them in his jar.

"Don't take the black ones," I said. "They're rotten."

"Uh-huh," he said, but continued doing it.

"They'll turn your skin black."

"No they won't."

"Where do you think black people come from?"

He squinted one eye in the sun. "From New Orleans?"

As that could've been true for all I knew, I shrugged, cracked one pecan against another, and picked out the meat. "Here's a good one. Want it?"

He shook his head. He actually didn't eat pecans all that much; he was more of a collector. He also collected rocks from the gravel driveway and he'd put them in his mouth. I'm pretty sure he swallowed them sometimes, but chickens did that too, so I figured it wouldn't kill him.

I SAW THE DUST down the road long before I heard the car, then the rumble of the blue Buick as it drove over the cattle guard and up our long driveway. It was my Uncle Dan, who was tough looking with the scar on his face and his hair mowed off, but generally had a pocket full of candy—or he did before he left one time and didn't come back. The mud-caked Buick Roadmaster crunched to a stop next to the fence. Uncle Dan's window was open, and he grinned at us. A woman I'd never seen before was sitting next to him, real close, and she had her arm draped over his shoulder.

"Hey there squirts," he said.

I didn't say anything because of that woman. With her short red hair and eyes the color of new pears, she was the most beautiful woman I'd ever seen…except for the splotch on her neck. I couldn't help but stare at it. It reminded me of the worm-leech that had stuck to my leg once when we'd been swimming in Goose Lake and I'd screamed until Pawpaw burned it with his cigarette. Leeches could suck you to the bone if you let them.

My uncle and that woman were out of the car now, and she was sort of leaning against him. Her plaid skirt fluttered in the breeze, just over her knees. She was barefoot like us, and I'd never seen a lady outside without shoes. Her toenails were painted green like her eyes, and I'd never seen that either.

"Charlie, Jute, I want you boys to meet your new aunt. You can call her Lona."

I tried to say something but my tongue had gotten so oyster-thick it filled my mouth. Jute didn't say anything either; I always did the talking for both of us, as he was only four and therefore stupid.

"Why, aren't you two a couple of *angels,*" Lona said. "Just a precious couple of heavenly *angels!*" She leaned down and pinched Jute on the cheek.

"Ow," Jute cried, and we both took a step back to avoid her pinchers.

"Don't hurt them now, Lona, they're just skin and nerves." Uncle Dan sort of chuckled. "Doesn't that memaw of yours feed you anything?"

I shrugged. "Rice and syrup."

"Here," he said, reaching in his pocket and producing a handful of Bazooka bubblegum pieces, "these'll put some muscle on yah."

We each grabbed some, Uncle Dan scruffed my hair, then he and Aunt Lona headed for the house. Aunt Lona was having trouble walking, and Uncle Dan was kinda of holding her up. When they got to the steps I remembered and yelled, "Watch out for the ants!"

Uncle Dan glanced back and winked, and they headed up as if they didn't have a care in the world. I ran to the steps just as the screen door snapped behind them—no ants now, just the sugary stain of Jute's root beer, already dried.

2

JUTE AND ME WENT on collecting pecans. When we came back to the house, two huge velvets were on the stairs and naturally Jute wouldn't go near it.

"Jump over them like I did."

He just stood there, stringy bits of gum stuck to his face. His Bazooka Joe comic had fallen in the dirt, but he hadn't noticed. I didn't have shoes on, and I couldn't use the jar to bash them 'cause Memaw said if I broke another one I wouldn't be sitting for a week, so I went on inside.

The cigar smoke was thick in there, smelling of cherries and burning hay. The adults were in the living room, talking. A football game was flickering on the new color TV. That TV had cost so much Pawpaw had turned the color knob all the way, squeezing out every bit of value he could get. The grass on the screen was as green as the algae that plugged up Jute's nose one time. All the other colors were like that—so bright they scorched your eyes.

"There's ants," I said, but nobody looked at me except Lona. She smiled with all her teeth, then looked back at Pawpaw. He was telling a story in French, but I could tell she didn't understand it. I didn't either, if you want to know the truth. The old governor said those who spoke French weren't as good as those who spoke English, so best kids didn't learn it. So I didn't. Not learning came easy to me.

"Jute froze up," I said, louder this time. "'Cause of the ants."

"Just step on them, squirt. They don't bite." Uncle Dan said this without looking at me, then burst out laughing. They all did. Maybe Pawpaw was telling a joke, but I couldn't tell. I looked at the painting behind him. My mother Marla had done it with oil paints on a rice sack. It had a mountain of pure white rocks. I'd never seen mountains in real life…or rocks either, not big ones like those, anyway. I wondered if those rocks had really looked like that, bright and shiny like diamonds. Then I went upstairs to get my Buster Browns. I didn't wear them much, just for going to school and to church on Sunday, and for killing bugs.

After dinner, I helped Memaw wash the dishes in the sink—along with the pistol she washed every Sunday. I asked her where Aunt Lona came from with a mark on her neck like that, and she said never mind where she came from. All I needed to know was Uncle Dan and Aunt Lona would be staying with us for a while, so I'd have to give up my room and sleep with Jute. I said I wouldn't because Jute peed in the bed, but she said I would or I could live in the barn with the tractors and snakes. I said fine, I'd take the snakes. But the more I thought about those snakes slithering over my legs at night—rat snakes and corn snakes and hognose snakes, thousands of them fighting to get to me—the more a little pee in the bed didn't seem so bad. Besides, I figured I could get Jute to freeze up mid-pee if I beat him.

Dan

WHILE JUTE AND CHARLIE were playing in the field, Dan and Lona were upstairs in Charlie's room—their room now. Dan was thinking how odd to be in Red Church again. Some sort of mental geography drove people in circles, he decided. Even the world was set up like that—if you tried to go in a straight line, you'd just loop around and end up where you started.

Right back in Red Church. A nothing town, one foot above sea level...if that much.

He'd lived in real towns—New Orleans and Houston, even got as far north as Fairbanks once, but thought he'd freeze to death, and almost did. He'd spent far too much time in Kansas City (a stay that came with free room and board, courtesy of the Missouri Department of Corrections), and now here he was, circled back home, the first place anyone with intelligence would look for a person.

Lona was lounging on the bed, reading a brand new Bible, and he was sitting on a chair with worn-out green upholstery, admiring her. For one thing, she had no clothes on, and for another, she was fairly covered up with freckles, even a big one on her neck that looked like a worm. Like something you'd use for bait. He'd never tell her that, though, not unless he wanted to be rid of her; she was sensitive about it. Still, he had a devil inside that wanted to say something, and he always told him, don't be a jackass, devil Dan.

"You're thinking up a storm over there," she said as she turned a page.

"No I ain't."

"Well, you're doing something."

"I'm just looking."

"That's what I like about you, Dan Boone."

"What's that?"

"That you'll just sit there and look at me, like I'm the centerfold in Playboy."

"You could be, you know. You're just as pretty as any of those bunnies."

She touched her birthmark with a finger, then turned a page. Dan knew that magazines had artists who could airbrush out pubic hair and moles, even extra titties or heads if you had them. They could make hump noses straighter and short legs longer, and make just about any woman perfect. But he didn't say any of that, of course. Instead, he got up and looked out the window. His brother Landry's weedy kids were out there in the pasture. Charlie was bareback on the old mare, and Jute was standing on a stump. Charlie was trying to pull him up, finally managing to get him lying across the horse's rump like a squirming bedroll.

The horse started off through the pasture, slow and gentle. Dan had ridden that horse when he was Charlie's age, so how old was Lunch Time now? Twenty? Twenty-one? He pulled his t-shirt over his head and dropped it on the chair, then enjoyed the slanting sun on his chest for a moment before sliding on the bed alongside Lona, who moved over to make room for him.

Dan could make out just a little of what she was reading, which didn't sound much like the Bible: …*he pressed into her hard. His stomach slapped hers, again and again, and against her will she moaned, a primeval sound that surprised her, an animal cry that*—

She turned the page, and with one hand, pressed down into the looseness of his jeans. Soon she dropped the book off the side of the bed, and they continued where the book left off.

4

ABOUT A WEEK AFTER Uncle Dan and Aunt Lona moved in, Lona took me to my school in Red Church. We said we lived in Red Church, but really we didn't. About a thousand people lived there so it was pretty big, even if not as big as New Iberia, which was about twice as big but took most of an hour to get to. I rode up in front, and every time Lona came to a turn she'd stomp on the brake and put out her hand to catch me, then she'd turn around and check on Jute, who was holding onto the door handle for dear life.

"You're not going to open that door and fall out?" she asked him.

He just shook his head without saying anything, so I said, "No ma'am, he fell out once, and he's not gonna do it again."

She looked at me and grinned. "You don't have to call me ma'am. I told you that."

"No ma'am, I know it."

"I'm not much older than you. Not really."

"Yes ma'am."

"Just call me Lona."

"Yes ma'am, I surely will."

She shook her head, reached in her purse for her pack of cigarettes. She handed them to me and asked me to fire one up for her, which I did. I pushed in the lighter, and when it popped out, I tapped the red-hot end of it to one end of the cig while I sucked on the other. I liked that she trusted me to do things that grown people did, and I inhaled some each time I lit one. I figured the smoke would toughen up my lungs. That's what Uncle Dan said, that smoking gave you strong lungs, and I wanted to be strong so I could beat up Mousey Bertrand.

Mousey was the son of my teacher, Mrs. Bertrand. "That Mousey," I heard her say one day, "he's going to be a doctor, you watch. A baby doctor." She was probably right about that 'cause he was always pulling boys' pants down in the bathroom. Wanting to examine their privates.

"Looks like you got pus down there," he'd say. "You been playing with that? 'Cause if you been playing with that, it might have'ta come off."

If anyone was worth beating up, it was him. I figured he didn't have somebody to give him cigarettes, so his days of playing doctor at Red Church Elementary were numbered.

"Charlie?" Lona said as we passed the falling-down sign that said "Red Church, 1 mile."

"Ma'am?"

"You learn your spelling words?"

"Yes ma'am. Black, roof, chair, table."

"All right, how do you spell 'table'?"

"Oh, ah…I can't do that right now."

"You just said you knew how to spell it."

"I can't just spell it in my head. I got to have a pencil."

"I can spell it," Jute said from the backseat. "c-a-t."

I looked back there. Jute had his nose up against the door, his hand sticking out in the air, playing airplane. "How come he's coming with us? He doesn't go to school."

"Maybe if I leave him something will happen. You don't want something to happen, do you?"

"I don't know, sometimes. When he pees in the bed."

She puffed on her cigarette, not looking at me. "Are you mad we took your bed?"

"No ma'am," I said, but actually I was. Who liked waking up to the smell of pee? I'd tried to stay awake so I could catch him doing it, but that was harder than I thought.

"Jeez Louise," Lona said. She cut the wheel and we almost went into the ditch. I slid on the seat and bumped into her, just as a truck flew by. It had a yellow light on the roof. "I thought he was after me."

"That's just the Esso truck," I said as I moved back to my side. "Hank Leigh's dad drives it."

Lona rubbed her face, then got back on the road. She'd looked happy before, but now she seemed worried, and she didn't say a thing till we got to school. "Your memaw will be back this afternoon. She'll pick you up."

"Okay," I said.

5

NOBODY HAD EVER TALKED TO ME as much as Dan and Lona, and that might be why I got to thinking more than usual. Of course, thinking in school was not a good thing. You're supposed to be learning, not wasting your time thinking. But here I was, thinking about the black man down the block when I was supposed to be coloring on my coloring paper. Through the window I saw him kneeling on a roof, hammering on nails, and every time his hammer came down, it banged when it was already back in the air. I asked Mrs. Bertrand about it, which was a mistake; she generally got mad every time I asked her anything that wasn't in our books. This time she said I was too young to ask such questions. "You'll learn science in the fifth grade. You can ruin your brain if you don't learn things in the proper sequence."

"Did you learn things in the sea quench?" I asked, like I actually knew what a sea quench was.

She looked at me as if I'd spit on her shoes, then grabbed up my paper and held it out to me. "What do you call this? Where did you get these colors anyway? They are just all wrong."

"They are?"

"The sky isn't green; it's blue. And rocks aren't white; they're brown. Rocks are supposed to be brown!"

"No ma'am, I seen them. Sometimes rocks are pure white."

"I saw them."

"Uh-huh. White like diamonds."

"I *saw* them. The verb is saw, not seen."

"Oh."

"I swear. You Boone children are destined for prison. There's no accounting why, and there's nothing to be done to save you."

"Yes'm."

I guess she was talking abut my dad, who'd gone up the river for a spell—to the penitentiary in Angola—and I wondered if Mrs. Bertrand had been his teacher too. She looked old enough. Her mouth was all wrinkled and she had flat teeth like a mule. She was grinding them together just like an old mule chewing a carrot.

"You have mule teeth," I said before I could stop myself. That didn't do a thing but get me sent to the office to get spanked by Mr. Oday Faat, the principal. He'd played baseball at LSU one year and had a good strong arm. He also had a paddling board with holes drilled in it that was made by a boy at the high school who drowned one Friday night. I forget the boy's name, but the paddle had its own name burned in the wood: *Board of Lower*

Education. I'd heard Mr. Faat had used that board twenty times a day for ten years and it wasn't even close to giving out. There was even a poem about it:

> *Mr. Faat gave me thirty whacks*
> *When he saw what he had done*
> *He gave me thirty-one*

Tim Guidry in my class wrote that. Mrs. Bertrand always said Tim was going to be a fine writer 'cause he was so original. Not me though. Memaw said I might want to take up counting, seeing how I counted everything. Counters made good money, she claimed. Right now I was counting the whacks.

"Charlie," he said after thirteen two-handed swings. "You about learned your lesson?"

"Uh-huh," I said, just glad to get through this without crying. As it was, I could hardly stand up straight.

"And next time you'll control that mouth of yours?"

"Yes sir, I surely will. Next time I'll ask my uncle if I want to know something's not in the book."

"That isn't what I…oh never mind." He hung the board on its nail. "So Dan Boone is back in town?"

"Uh-huh. He and my aunt Lona."

"He got married, did he?" Mr. Faat looked out the dirty window that had chicken wire in it, stroking his skinny chin.

"I guess."

"You guess?"

"I never asked him exactly. But they sleep in my room."

"And where do you sleep?"

"I sleep with Jute. He'll be coming to school before long."

"Ah yes, another notch for the board."

"Sir?"

"Nothing. About time you get back to class." I had my hand on the doorknob when he said, "I probably should write a note to your granddad, but this time I won't. This is just between you and me, Charlie. Just this once, okay?"

I nodded. I was thankful not to get another note, not that Pawpaw ever took them serious. He'd just shake his head, saying, "You getting to be just like your dad."

6

Memaw picked me up after school. She was driving the old Ford Standard that wasn't much good because Pawpaw was always taking the tires off and putting them on again. We were headed home when the seat kinda gave way, and I grabbed onto the door handle. A terrible noise came from the back, screeching and scratching. About then I saw a tire rolling along side of us, which didn't seem right.

"I don't believe it," Memaw said as she jerked the steering wheel and guided the car onto the dirt that bordered the road. The tire kept on going by itself and finally fell over in the ditch. We got out and looked after it.

"I'll kill him for this," Memaw said.

"You want me to get it?" I said.

"You know how to put a tire on?"

"Yes ma'am, I sure do. I saw Pawpaw do it lots of times."

"You didn't saw him, Charlie."

"I didn't?"

"You saw wood with a saw, not people."

"Oh."

"You learning anything in that school?"

"Uh-huh, most every week." I thought of Mrs. Bertrand growing up in Lake Charles like she'd said one time, and I thought how strange to grow up in a lake and learn from a sea quench. By now I pictured quenches with eyes the size of hubcaps and sixteen arms. Pink, flailing arms. And Mrs. Bertrand with her mule teeth, underwater with the quenches.

Memaw lit a cigarette with a match, then looked up and down the parish road, where not a car was in sight. "All right, Charlie. Let's see what Pawpaw taught you about tires. It'll be like a test."

I frowned as I didn't like tests much, but I took off running and soon was rolling the tire back to the car. I even got the back end jacked up like you're supposed to do, and got the tire mounted on the axle. And that's when I realized all the nuts were gone, and the tire wouldn't stay on without nuts, which is why it fell off to begin with.

"Does this mean I failed the test?" I said.

"No honey," she said. "You did your best."

About then a mud-spattered Pontiac passed going the other way, and the man driving glanced back at us. I didn't know him but he slowed and finally stopped far down the road. After he just sat there for several minutes, Memaw started wondering if he was going to help us or what. I said maybe he'd run out of gas and was waiting for us to help him.

"Not likely," she said. She waved a white handkerchief and

he finally began backing up. He stopped, though, still a good distance away.

"What's he doing?" I said.

What he was doing came clear a moment later when the driver's door sprung open and a naked man stepped out. My skin went cold, and I just stared at him coming toward us. I figured he wasn't going to help us with the tire.

Memaw got back in the car. I thought she didn't want to look 'cause he was naked, but no, she was just getting something from her purse. A paper bag, and in it, the pistol that she washed in the sink even though Pawpaw said that was no way to clean a gun. She got out and straight away began shooting bullets, no warning or nothing. The man began yelling in French and waving his hands, then turned and took off running. I think she hit him in the leg because he began limping and sort of fell in his car. She shot once more as he was driving off and his rear window exploded. The car slid from one side of the road to the other, and soon was out of sight.

Memaw slipped the gun back into its paper bag, the bag back in her purse, then turned to me. "Charlie, what you saw here is what happens to bad people. If anyone does something like this, you do what you have to do, you hear me?"

"I guess."

"There's no guessing about it. You go ahead and shoot him. Jesus will understand, okay?"

I nodded.

"If he dies, it's just between Father Martel and yourself. No one else has to know."

And she didn't mention it to Pawpaw either, though she let him have it when we got home. He wasn't to fool around with the tires anymore; he was to take the car to the Esso station like normal people, now that we had all that money Uncle Dan gave us. He didn't say anything, just suffered her words while looking at his shoes. I guess he felt the way I did when Mrs. Bertrand told me how stupid I was.

Once Memaw stomped off to the house, Pawpaw said, "She probably thinks I did it on purpose."

"She didn't say nothing like that."

"Uh-huh." He looked over at the car. "Tell me, Charlie, if all the nuts fell off, how did y'all ever get it home?"

"I took a nut from the other tires, so every tire had four nuts instead of five. Except for the tire that fell off and I put bubble-gum on that one."

"They're wheels, not tires. The tire is just the rubber part."

"Yes sir, I guess that's right."

"Anyway, weren't you afraid *all* the wheels would fall off?"

"A little. But then I remembered how most everything in the house is missing something or other, and it don't seem to make much difference."

Pawpaw smiled then, and winked at me. "That might be truer than you know."

7

DAN AND LONA WERE GONE for most of the week to sell their books—the trunk of their car was full of them. When I asked Memaw if they were coming back, she said she supposed. Which wasn't a very good answer. I liked my bed, liked not having pee in it. But Memaw said I had to be patient, Jute would grow out of this in time.

Assuming I didn't drown before that happened.

I went upstairs and opened the door of the room I'd lost. It had a dormer window that looked over the back field. I saw old Lunch Time grazing out there, looking like the most swayback creature in existence. Eating dandelions, which were her favorite. I lay on the bed and smelled the sheets. They had a strange smell, like from a far-away country. I got up and went through the drawers. The bottom drawer still had my stuff in it—socks and underwear, but all the others were filled with women's stuff, except one half of a drawer that had Uncle Dan's cigars, t-shirts, and boxer shorts. The stack was humped up on one side so I lifted it and found a box of bullets in there. Sure Shot, .38 caliber, it said. I opened the box. Eighteen of the bullets were gone. I figured he wouldn't miss just one, so I took one and put it in my pocket. Then I took another. Then another two. Most everything in the house was missing something, I figured, and nobody cared. I thought of taking one of the cigars, and even had it in my pocket, but then put it back in its box. Then I put it in my pocket again. Smoking a cigar would toughen up my lungs faster than anything. Tough Lung Charlie, they'd call me.

I passed Memaw on the way down the stairs.

"You weren't in your uncle's room, were you?"

"I just peeked inside. I sure did like it when I could sleep by myself."

"Nobody in this house gets to sleep by themselves, much as some would like to."

I could see how true that was.

In the barn I took out a yellowed newspaper clipping from my pocket and pressed it flat, reading it for the forty-eighth time:

MAN WHO LOST THUMB SENTENCED

A Red Church man who lost his right thumb during an attempted robbery of Frankie's Market has been sentenced to fifteen years hard labor. Circuit Judge Jay Neely sentenced Landry Alphonse Boone, 26, on Saturday, saying he had never seen a more useless human being in his entire legal career, and if he could lock up Boone's offspring along with him, the parish would be a safer place in the long run.

The judge's remarks came in response to Public Defender D.T. Abate's plea that Mr. Boone's two small boys needed him.

The judge also rejected the defendant's plea for leniency because of his injuries, noting that they resulted from firing a stolen pistol at a combination safe in Frankie's Market. Boone was apparently unaware that this gun had been spiked with a steel rod, and the explosion tore into Mr. Boone's hand, removing his thumb and part of his index finger. With Mr. Boone rolling on the floor, "wailing like a polecat," the owner of Frankie's Market entered, snuck up on Mr. Boone and beat him senseless with a can of Crisco.

The stolen "Bunch" gun, which had killed the notorious editor turned train robber, Eugene Bunch, has been returned to the Red Church History Museum on Lee Street, just across from Frankie's Market. Admission is twenty-five cents, Tuesdays through Fridays.

I folded up the clipping, hoping that Uncle Dan wouldn't make the same mistake my father had made, that he wouldn't get maimed by some museum gun.

8

Dan

"I LIKE THE LEATHER," said the minister's wife.

"It's Mongolian yak skin," Dan Boone said. Which was a lie, of course, but little about this Bible was legitimate, and Dan had been careful to direct the minister to those parts that were.

"This lettering," the minister said, fingering the inlaid, bronze-colored paint. "Is this gold?"

"Thirty-six carats," Lona said.

The minister looked up at her. "I thought twenty-four carat was pure gold?"

Dan didn't bat an eye. "That used to be true during the war."

"Eh?"

"Rationing, what I was told."

"Maybe so…I seem to remember that." The minister held the Bible to his nose, then hefted it in one hand. "Ten dollars, you say."

"Ten dollars, right, and that's dirt cheap. Especially when you consider that even a hundred for a book of this quality is far too little."

"Our last Bibles were five."

"Well yes, but—"

"Genesis fell out in a year."

"There, you see! You get what you pay for. Tijuana Bibles will last a lifetime—that's guaranteed. We package the good word with the finest materials. Pine saplings cut from the grounds of the governor's mansion in Missouri. Glue made from Kentucky derby winners."

"It is a beautiful book," the minister's wife said.

"Our founder desired that the faithful study His words surrounded by beauties, regardless of their station in life. So they could read this Bible in a bathroom and imagine they were in the Sistine Chapel."

The minister snorted. "The Vatican! A bottomless pit of iniquity."

Devil Dan was about to say something unfortunate when Lona cut in and saved him. "I always thought it was an evil place."

This seemed to mollify the old man, who almost smiled. He again opened the book and brought the pages to within an inch of his nose, which Dan now realized was to see it, not to sniff it. "Your founder wasn't a priest, was he?"

"Our founder was not a man of the cloth," Dan said, "but a man of paper and ink. This was his gift to the world, bless his soul." Dan made the sign of the cross. Lona and the minister's wife did the same, but the minister had his nose in Leviticus and didn't seem to notice.

"He walked in the footsteps of Gideon," Lona added.

The minister lowered the Bible to study her, and Dan knew that, if he could see anything at all, he was looking at the birthmark on Lona's neck. Except Lona had used a ballpoint to turn it into a cross.

"Gideon heard the word of God," the minister said, "without need for any book." Then he quoted: "So Gideon took them down to the water. There the Lord told him, separate those who lap water with their tongues like a dog from those who kneel down to drink."

"That's a fine passage," Dan said. "That Gideon sure knew about dogs, didn't he, Lona?" Dan was praying that the minister was as blind as he seemed, for he'd now flipped to the story of Solomon, which was illustrated with drawings of cavorting erotica that Dan could see from the sofa. "Lona, I said isn't that right?"

"Yeah…yeah, Gideon knew his dogs," she said, and Dan saw her working her magic on him, crossing and uncrossing her legs, licking her lips.

"Gideon's dogs," Dan said, "they were really great dogs."

"Our founder had four of them," Lona said.

The minister closed the Bible on his knees and placed both hands over it. "This founder, what did you say his name was?"

"Crumb," Lona said. "Felonious Crumb. My dear cousin, bless his soul. First cousin, twice removed. He was a saint. An absolute angel with a pen."

"I knew that from looking at you," the minister's wife said, beaming. "Because you too have such saintly features." They went off in that pleasant vein, even as the minister seemed to be building a head of steam about something.

"No need for a jury in these parts," he said suddenly.

The women went silent and Dan jerked in his chair. "What's that?"

"My wife can sense the good in people, and also the evil. I sometimes think she'll be given that job by Saint Peter, dividing the saints from the sluts. Casting bitches into the pit of perdition."

"Oh Tubble," his wife said, her cheeks now splotched with color. "Must you use such language?"

"If we pluck not the tails of bitches," he boomed, slapping the Bible on his knee, "they will defecate in our midst."

"Of course," Dan said. "We wouldn't want that." He noticed Lona tapping her wrist. Right, he thought, let's wind this up before something goes screwy. Now he had to deal with the issue he'd been putting off—that they didn't have the hundred books this customer wanted, and no way to get more any time soon. He picked up the sales ledger and ran his finger down a line at random, mumbling to himself.

The minister looked from Dan to Lona, then back to Dan. "Eh? Is there a problem?"

Dan tapped the page. "There might be a *slight* difficulty."

The minister's wrinkled eyes narrowed into slits.

"It's not really much of anything, actually. No reason for alarm. It's just that, we have only four dozen books in the car. It's been such a popular edition."

"Four dozen, forty-eight…"

"Well, forty-nine with the one you have there, which is near enough for half your congregation."

"I see."

"And of course, the cost would be half."

"Half the money for half the books?"

"That's right. Which would be—"

"Five dollars a book."

Damn! This minister was either an idiot or a rascal, and Dan soon began to suspect the latter. He settled in for what became an extended period of negotiations in which several glasses of lemonade were fetched by the minister's wife and set before him, each with a sprig of mint and a growing taste of alcohol. Rubbing alcohol, most likely, as Dan doubted they had any real drinking stuff in the house. He had developed a great tolerance for industrial chemicals in prison, but by degrees he became worried that they might manage to murder him anyway. Through an open doorway he noticed a box on the kitchen counter, the bright colors the same as ACME insecticide. One teaspoon of the stuff, he knew, could be fatal. He knew because he'd shared a cell with a Mormon who had a cemetery in his backyard—fourteen graves of traveling salesmen he'd poisoned. But he wasn't in there for murder, no indeed. For bigamy.

Dan began to sweat.

"Six," he said suddenly, and Lona looked at him with disappointment.

"Five," said the minister, who had not budged in all this time.

"All right then."

After a damp handshake sealed the deal, the minister fetched a cigar box from a back room and tediously counted out two hundred and forty-five dollars, the better part of that sum in ones. Dan filled out a receipt and the minister took the box along with the receipt into the bedroom. Dan craned his neck, but couldn't see around the half-closed door. The minister was hiding his cigar box under the bed, or perhaps under a board, and Dan wondered how much more might be in there.

When the minister returned, Dan tried to reopen negotiations for the next batch of Bibles, but was forced to submit by a glass of pure rubbing alcohol. Even so, five dollars was twice what he'd finagled in Shreveport from a Holy Roller who wasn't as blind or as devious as this one.

"You drive a hard bargain," Dan said. "Perhaps when the time comes, you could negotiate for me with Saint Peter?"

"Every man must pay full price for his sins," the minister snapped. "No one can Jew down the Lord."

"Amen," said his wife.

"Amen," Dan mumbled, suspecting he was right.

The minister's wife and their hulking son went out with Dan and Lona to fetch the Bibles from their car. Dan had just taken out the second box of twenty-four Bibles when a wail came from the house, like a man both killing and being killed. Then another wail, even more murderous than the last. A moment later the minister burst through the front door, his face apoplectic, bellowing like a madman: "Cursed pornographers! Damned filth from New Orleans!"

"Oh no!" his wife cried, clapping her hands together.

"Jonas!" he cried to his son, "drop that box of dung!"

"Tubble?" his wife said. "What's wrong?"

"What's wrong! What's wrong! We've been hoodwinked by reprobates!"

"Now Reverend," Dan began.

"Hold your tongue, you fiend. You can tell your lies to the judge."

The minister spun around for the house, but in his excitement lost his balance and tumbled backward off the porch. Lying unmoving in the dirt, face up, Dan first thought he was dead, but no, for he began cough and sputter, and then began yelling. Yelling for his son to shoot these dogs, these damnable pornographers. His son knelt next to him, but the old man shouted in his face and began hitting the boy on the arm. Finally, after a crunching blow to his ear, the boy stumbled up and ran into the house, the screen door snapping behind him.

In the midst of this tumult, Dan had tossed the abandoned boxes of Bibles into the open trunk and slammed it shut. He and Lona jumped in the front seat and they were rolling, the Roadmaster's tires scratching hard at gravel. They made it to the end of the driveway just as the son got back to the porch, armed with a rifle.

"Destroy them, boy!" bellowed the minister, who now was sitting up with the help of his wife. "Shoot those dogs with old Nellie!" Nellie was the name of the gun, apparently, the Great War souvenir that had long rusted on the mantle in their sitting room.

Gravel crunched. Grackles flew up from the cornfield along the road, blackening the sky. Dan threw the Buick into second. Past the gate now, Lona was laughing. She was beautiful when she laughed, Dan thought, and the wad of cash in her hands was even more beautiful.

A red-haired Madonna with a presidential bouquet.

This vision was destroyed in an instant when he glanced in the rearview. The boy was pointing that German relic at him, and the minister was crying, "Shoot them! Shoot them!" A smoke ring burped from its muzzle and a bullet cut the air, squalling by Dan's window. Then two more cut into the trunk, thundering like great hammer blows. Lona squealed and ducked, dropping the wad of cash. George Washingtons swirled around in the car.

"Dammit!" Dan cried, for the day was ruined; their profit had flown out the window.

9

Jute and me were just inside the barn, and I had a rock on a rusty sprocket, ready to hit it with a hammer. I'd set the sprocket on bricks in the doorway so it'd be in the light.

Clop.

A spark flew and the rock crumbled, but I didn't see any crystals inside. Sometimes the rocks were hollow and had purple crystals—what a boy in my class said were the petrified boogers of Adam and Eve. Of course that was a lie, 'cause no way Eve left any boogers. There weren't even any desks to leave boogers under. Not in the Garden of Eden.

"Let me try," Jute said.

"In a minute." I took one of those bullets from my pocket and put it on the sprocket.

"That's a bullet?" Jute said. "Can I see it?"

"You can see it fine where it is."

"I want to hold it."

"Nope."

"Why not, Charlie?"

"Because you'll put it in your mouth."

"No I won't."

"And then you'll swallow it. Bullets are too expensive to swallow."

"Why are they expensive?"

"'Cause of the lead. Lead is expensive."

"What's the lead?"

"It's the gray stuff there."

"Is it the yellow part?"

"Nope. That's the brass."

"I like the yellow part."

"Shows how much you know. Lead's twice as expensive."

"Huh."

"That's why I'm getting it. Now stand back. I might have to move fast to catch it."

Jute took a step back, but he was leaning so much that his head hadn't moved much at all. I took a swing at the bullet and Jute jumped back at the noise. It had frightened him, and he looked like he was ready to cry. Worse, the lead was gone, and the brass part was kinda flattened.

"It's gone," he said. "Where'd it go?"

I didn't know, but I wasn't about to admit it. "You were in my way so I couldn't see where it went."

"Was not."

"Look around. Maybe it fell in the dirt."

The ground was littered with hay and powdered manure. Jute

got down close and finally picked up a bit of broken rock. "Is this it?"

I shook my head, then pulled another bullet from my pocket. "Looks like this," I said. He tried to grab it, but I snatched it away. "Nope, you'll just swallow it."

"I said I won't."

"Uh-huh. You just stand there and watch. This time I wanna see where it goes."

"Why don't you put your hand over it and catch it?"

I shook my head. "I think it might come out kinda fast."

"As fast as a baseball?"

"Even faster."

"That could hurt."

"Yep, so stand back now. And keep your eyes open." I swung the hammer, and *bang*, the same thing happened, except I saw something hit the car. "I think it's over there." We ran over to Pawpaw's car, and sure enough, we found a hole in the passenger door, right in the middle.

"Is that it?" Jute said.

"I think it's in there."

Jute dug a finger in, then tried to see inside. "How you gonna get it?"

I opened the door and studied the red fabric panel that had turned tan at the top. "We might have to take this apart."

"How you gonna do that?"

I pointed at a screw. "This is a Phillips head. If you want to get in something, you take it out."

An hour later the sun was really bearing down on us, so Jute got in the backseat. I was sweating, using a screwdriver to get out the last of the long screws—all ten of them. When I did the fabric popped out a bit and the window fell into the door with a clunk. I turned the handle, but the window wouldn't come up. We both looked at it, then at each other.

"Is that supposed to happen?" Jute said.

"I don't think so."

"You broke it."

"It's not broke."

"You gonna get whipped, Charlie."

"I know how to put it back."

"And you made that hole in the door."

"I didn't. The bullet did that."

"You gonna get whipped anyhow. Pawpaw is gonna whip you so bad."

I sighed, and as the fabric panel still wouldn't come out, I started putting the screws back in. Truth was, I liked Jute a lot better when he didn't talk. And now how he talked! He kept me up half the night, reminding me in case I forgot.

"Gonna get whipped," he'd say, and then giggle to himself. Finally I told him to shut up or I'd say he did it. "Uh-uh," he said. "You can't say that 'cause it's a lie."

"Doesn't matter. They'll believe me anyway." Then I told him the whole story like he'd done it, and I didn't hear a peep out of him for the rest of the night.

10

THE NEXT MORNING I woke to a slam of a door, and I saw that the closet door was shut, which it never was because Jute had to see that it wasn't full of monsters. The smell of perfume and pee was heavy in the air, which didn't much smell like the muck-stench of monsters.

"Is somebody in there?" I asked.

Not a sound. I threw back the sheet, which was stained yellow on Jute's side. Jute was sitting up, his eyes as big as bowls.

"Is somebody in that closet?" I said again.

"It's the monster," Jute whispered.

"I got a gun," I said. "I'll shoot a hole in the door if you don't come out."

"He will too," Jute said.

"Nobody's in here," came a woman's voice.

"Aunt Lona?"

Nothing.

"I need to get my clothes."

"Put on your old clothes," she said.

"Oh…okay."

I put on the jeans and checkered shirt from the day before and then looked out the window. The sheriff was out there with Pawpaw, looking over Uncle Dan's car, which hadn't been there the day before.

"That's the sheriff," Jute said from behind me, wearing only his half-yellow underwear.

"I know it is."

"He's gonna arrest you."

"Why don't you go wash that pee off? It stinks."

"It don't stink." Still, he looked down, frowned, then went flatfooted out the door.

I turned back to the window and watched Pawpaw point to the back door of his own car. They both squatted there and studied it. I had an ice-pick feeling in the pit of my stomach, like I did when they fed us that green chicken at school that they thought would be fine if they seasoned it enough.

I went out and down the hall. Jute was in the bathroom, and I could hear him in there talking to himself and laughing, probably at the thought of me getting arrested so he could pee on both sides of the bed. I went on to Uncle Dan's room—my old room—and knocked. Nobody knew how to get out of a tight spot as good as my uncle.

"Uncle Dan?"

No answer.

I knocked again. "Uncle Dan? You in there?" The door opened

a bit. A hand reached out, grabbed my arm and pulled me in. "Unc—"

"Shhhh," Uncle Dan whispered. "The goddamn sheriff is here." I'd never seen him scared before, but now he was. It reminded me of my daddy, 'cause the sheriff came for him too.

"I saw him out the window," I said. "He and Pawpaw are out there looking at holes."

"Shit."

"He's here to arrest me."

"Arrest you? How come?"

"'Cause I made that hole in the car."

Uncle Dan let out some air and went limp, sat back on the bed. "Don't worry about that, Charlie. It already had a hole."

"It did?"

"Two of them. Had a little run-in with a homicidal preacher over by Leesville. He might've finished off that old Buick—and us too—if his son hadn't been cockeyed."

"It weren't your car. It was Pawpaw's car."

"You put a hole in Pawpaw's car?"

"Uh-huh."

"How'd you do that?"

"With a bullet."

"You *shot* your granddad's car?"

"Uh-huh."

"Where'd you get the gun?"

"I didn't have a gun."

"You didn't have a gun."

"I shot it with a hammer."

Uncle Dan snorted. Then he put his hands on my shoulders

and looked at me seriously. "Charlie, I want you to do something for Lona and me."

I said I would.

He said first off not to worry about the hole. They wouldn't know I'd made it unless I told them, and I wasn't that stupid, was I? (I said I wasn't.) But the sheriff was up to no good, Uncle Dan was certain of that, so he wanted me to sneak out there and listen to that "goddamned sheriff and Pawpaw," and I was to remember everything they said and report back, like I was a spy. A Confederate spy behind Union lines. But I wasn't to say anything or draw attention to myself, or to let on that he and Aunt Lona were in the house. I said Aunt Lona was in the closet in mine and Jute's room, and he said that was fine, just go out there do what he asked.

THE FRONT DOOR OF THE HOUSE was open, and I saw that Memaw was out there with the men—all three adults standing next to the sheriff's car, talking about those holes, I figured. As I crept down the steps, I was lucky to see the red velvet in time. I jumped over it, right onto the corner of a half-buried brick. "Ow," I cried as I rolled around, holding my foot. "Dang it," I said, "gosh dang it," though my aim was not to say anything at all, and surely not to curse like that.

11

I DIDN'T GET ARRESTED because the sheriff thought that high school kids probably made those holes, driving around, shooting up cars as high school students were wont to do on weekends. They'd shot up Maurice Leduc's car too. He was a cattle farmer we didn't know, and they shot out his window. I thought maybe he was the naked man who didn't help us with the tire, but I didn't say that to the sheriff. I figured that was between Memaw and Jesus, none of the sheriff's business. And anyway, she was staring at me so hard I was afraid to say a word.

The sheriff looked at her, then at me, and he said, "She's probably thinking you might turn out that way too, shooting up cars for fun. You wouldn't do that, now would you, Charlie?"

"No sir, not with a gun."

Which wasn't a lie, and that was good because I wouldn't have to confess it to Father Martel. I didn't much like him—half the

43

time he didn't make sense, and the other half he reminded me of Mousey Bertrand. Jute claimed to be sorry I wasn't arrested, but not Aunt Lona, who was so happy she fixed us eggs and bacon for breakfast, while singing "No Place Like Home," and we'd not had bacon for a real long time. I didn't ask her why she was in our closet, and Jute didn't either. If monsters lived in there, most anyone could.

Later that morning Pawpaw decided he'd discovered a "fact of nature," because when he took apart the door of his car, he found the bullet on the wrong side of the window glass, like it had passed through the glass without breaking it. He got the idea that bullets could pass through glass if the night was dark enough, and he talked about this until Memaw told him to shut up about it. After Memaw went to church in the car—which was now missing the back door—Pawpaw broke all the glasses from the kitchen doing experiments. He'd take Mason jars out to the barn, we'd hear the shots, and then he'd come back for more, saying he was getting close to the secret, just needed to get it a little darker. Uncle Dan encouraged him in this, saying Edison didn't succeed overnight—took him a thousand broken light bulbs before he got even one to work. Then he winked at me like a movie star. I asked him why he'd let his daddy break all the glasses in the house, and he said it kept the old boy happy.

Uncle Dan wasn't happy when he opened up his trunk, though. Those bullets had passed right through his boxes and punched a hole in every single Bible, even in the dark. His entire inventory, he said, had been killed off in an instant by a cross-eyed boy and his lunatic father. Never mind that those books had probably saved their lives, for their lives should never have been in danger. They were just selling Bibles to ministers, after all.

44

In such a holy transaction, gunfights were unseemly.

His mood improved after Lona said she had an even better plan for their employment—something she'd read about in the paper. She didn't tell us what it was, even though Uncle Dan said it was a real good idea. This time they'd bring home not only the bacon, he said, but enough pigs to fill up a poke.

I wasn't sure what a poke was, but Jute and me spent an hour making a list of names for the pigs that Uncle Dan would be bringing us. George Washington Boone was my favorite, along with George Washington Boone the second. Jute came up with Bee Bee and Billy Bog, which I told him were stupid names and I wouldn't write them down, and he said if I didn't know how to spell them he could tell me, and I said don't bother.

12

MONDAY MORNING I got into a fight during recess. Mousey Bertrand said us Boones didn't have enough sense or money to keep doors on our car—according to his father who smoked so much he spent most of Sunday service in the parking lot—and I said we did too and he said no we didn't, so I punched him in the face. He pulled my ear and I tore his shirt. We rolled around for a while and I got him pinned somehow, sitting on his back, and when the second tardy bell rang, all the onlookers went back to class—six boys and the Fontenot twins who were crying because Mousey had lost. Why girls liked boys was still a mystery to me, and why anyone liked Mousey was right up there with the holy mysteries I struggled with in catechism.

We were now late for class, but I continued to sit on Mousey, as he was bigger than me and I was afraid to let him up. A good ten minutes I sat on him (without spitting on his neck as he later claimed) before I saw his mother shaking her fist in a window and I finally let him go. I figured he'd run at me like a bull and wallop me good, but he didn't. He did a lot worse than that.

"You're a goddam hospital child," he yelled, using up every bit of his fifth grade vocabulary.

"I am not," I yelled back, even though I wasn't exactly clear on what it was. Hospital had never been on our spelling tests, even though I'd heard it used in hushed voices, 'cause people went there to have their innards cut out, after which they died, most of the time.

"You don't have no mama or daddy," Mousey yelled. "That makes you one. You ain't nothing but a hospital child and a bastard."

"I have grandparents," I said weakly. "Memaw and Pawpaw."

"They're bastards. They're all bastards. Your whole family is bastard."

He walked off then, his head held high with moral superiority, and I stared after him, knowing he'd be telling everyone I was a hospital child and a bastard. The devil roasted bastards on skewers, didn't he? And I sure couldn't imagine any hospital children invited to birthday parties or Fourth of July parties, except that hot one down in the bowels of the earth.

It got hot enough in Principle Faat's office. After the usual amount of talk, he paddled me twenty-seven times for fighting, thirteen times for ignoring the tardy bell, then sixteen times more for destruction of property—Mousey's torn-up shirt. And for the first time in his office, I cried real tears, burning tears that were icy on my cheeks.

I cried like a bastard.

13

Lona

LONA CONSIDERED that when you wanted food you went to a grocery, and when you wanted money you went to a bank. What could be more obvious than going to where they stocked what you wanted? So all this business of selling their Tijuana Bible inventory to penny-pinching ministers didn't make sense. Sure, it gave Felonious Crumb a bad name, but what good did that do? Of what profit was revenge, her father used to thunder. He was a minister himself, and he'd gone to jail for embezzling four thousand dollars of church funds. Four thousand seemed like a lot, but when Lona divided it by his fifteen year sentence, it came to about three cents an hour.

Less than minimum wage, even then.

DAN AND LONA WAITED their turn at the Great Southern Bank of Baton Rouge. Dan was near the front of the line, and the Texan ahead of him turned and asked the time. The Texan was wearing a fawn-colored felt hat and a watch that seemed to have stopped. He rapped it with a knuckle, then put it to his ear. Damn newfangled quartz watch, he said. Quartz wasn't nothing but a rock, so how could a watch run off a rock? Dan looked at his own watch—a wind-up Timex—and said it was just after one.

They soon got to discussing the big issues of the day as men do while standing in line when one of them has a broken watch. The relative economy of used cars versus new cars, the communist problem of Russia, the even worse problem of Cuba, and what Kennedy was going to do about those missiles. The Texan suggested we nuke the bastards and Dan said that might be bad for the financial system. Whatever, the man said. He was just hoping the crisis would spike the price of sugar, because he'd make a fortune. Sugar, he said, leaning over and whispering so loud everyone could hear him. Get in now, as Cuban sugar was history. Was that a fact, Dan wanted to know.

Lona tuned them out. She didn't like the way this Texan kept glancing back at her, looking her up and down, and she didn't care about sugar or cars or any of that other stuff. She was just glad that Dan's hair was coming back in. They'd buzzed it off when they locked him up, saying it was for lice control. But Dan was as clean as a banker. He didn't have any lice on him anywhere. Not a one. Now she nervously fingered the gun in her purse, hoping this wasn't going to be a terrible mistake.

14

I GUESS MOST BOYS don't think much about relatives and all that, and most boys I knew could barely tell you who their brothers and sisters were, much less their first cousins and their second cousins once removed—which I figured meant they'd gone somewhere and come back, like Uncle Dan. While I didn't know that sort of thing, I did know everybody's names, their real names. I always called my grandfather Pawpaw, but I knew his real name was Gustave, and Memaw's real name was Ezilda. Even though she usually called him Gus and he always called her Lidia. Lidia, because her mother had the same name and he didn't want to mix 'em up. Not that it mattered anymore, since Memaw's mother had been dead like a century, a longer time than I'd been alive. But I guess people get in a habit.

Gus and Lidia had three children: Centipede, who died as a little girl; Uncle Dan, who was the youngest; and my dad, who was the oldest. My dad was Landry Boone, and my mom was Marla Arsenault Boone—who they called Mary sometimes—but she blew away right after Jute was born. Memaw said she was taken up by Hurricane Iris, but I didn't believe it. A hurricane that could take you up in the sky to meet Jesus, I'd sure remember it.

At the kitchen table I mixed up my rice with fried okra, and asked Memaw why I didn't remember my mother flying away in a hurricane, and she said if I needed a mother I could do worse than Lona. She might be young, but she had a good heart, and she was going to heaven to meet my mother one day—along with us boys if we behaved ourselves and didn't turn out like my daddy and his brother Dan. Because they were going someplace else.

15

LONA'S PLAN was to make a withdrawal while the security guards were at the annual security workers appreciation luncheon—she'd read about the luncheon in the Baton Rouge *Daily Advocate*. The governor would be there, along with half the police force, since they moonlighted as security guards too. So a couple of nervy bank robbers could point their guns around like Clyde Barrow and Bonnie Parker, fill up a bag with as much money as they could carry, and disappear before dessert was served. People didn't argue with guns, not without armed men to back them up. Today the city of Baton Rouge was wide open for picking, fleecing, or just old fashioned helping yourself.

It didn't quite work out that easily, however, as the banks had brought in replacements. Dan and Lona had to try three banks before they found a security guard they thought they could handle. He wasn't much better than a cardboard cutout—about seventy and seemingly unarmed. Not to mention asleep. Even so, Dan had become squirrelly as they stood in line. He was dragging his feet; a gap had appeared before him, and Lona nudged him to go ahead.

"Look at him," she whispered, nodding toward the guard. "He's snoring."

"I don't hear anything."

"He is."

Dan studied the inert old man and bit his lip. "All right," he said finally. "But this ain't like I thought."

Now Dan was second in line. The man in front of him—the Texan who stood to make a killing from the Cuban missile crisis—glanced at the security guard, turned to the teller, and pulled out a gun.

"You're a pretty girl," he said. "If you want to stay that way, get the fuck back from the window and keep your hands where I can see them. All three of yah." The teller almost fell over herself as she retreated, joined by the two other, much older women. He tossed the girl a laundry bag. "Fill it up."

"I have to get to the counter for that," she said.

"No, no, no. Fill it from the cart." And, in fact, a cart had just arrived to replenish the teller stations. Paper wrapped bills were stacked up high.

On the other side of the counter, customers were backing away from the gunman, tripping over each other. A woman with a baby cried out repeatedly, "He's going to shoot us!" and her baby wailed every time.

"Shut up with that or I'll shoot you for sure." The Texan stepped over to the security guard and bent down. The guard snorted, his head lolled back. "Drunk," the Texan observed, then yelled in his ear, "You wasted, old man?" The guard didn't react, except for a white line of drool that trickled from his mouth. Tex turned back to the customers. "All right," he said. "You people against the wall over there…That's it. And put your hands up. Put 'em up. Put 'em up, goddammit!"

Dan and Lona had experience with putting their hands up, but this was new to a fat woman with a huge straw hat. Either the hat was too big or her arms were too heavy, but she was only able to flop them around until the Texan went over to her and plucked off her hat.

"That's my hat," she said.

"It's a stupid hat." He dropped it, and when she bent over to retrieve it, he stepped on it. "Just leave the damn thing and put your hands up."

"It cost me fourteen dollars." When she began tugging on the brim and pushing on his leg, he whacked her head with his pistol. She went down on her side like a horse. He kicked the hat and it rolled off across the white marble floor, trailing a silken stream of gladiolas. Lona watched this closely, as she saw this robber was experienced in his line of work.

He glanced at Lona, then down at her purse.

"Sir," said the cashier from behind him. "I filled your bag."

"Yeah, uh, leave it on the counter." He sidled over to the teller window, still looking at Lona. Grabbed the bag, glanced inside, then cinched it shut with the drawstring. "Everybody," he said, waving the gun, "everybody get on the floor, hands on your heads…except you, honey."

He came over to Lona, smirking. Everyone was lying face-down now, though Dan had one hand on his head and one hand inching toward his jacket pocket. The robber, correctly suspecting that Dan was up to no good, fired into the floor next to him. Chips of marble flew, the baby screeched, and Dan snatched his hand away and put it on his head. His watch was now next to his ear, the ticking so horribly loud that Dan wished it would stop.

The Texan now moved up closer to Lona, who had a big straw purse hanging from her shoulder, one hand now in it as though she had something in there she didn't want him to see.

"You can't let go that fat ole deposit, can you sweetheart?"

"I don't know what you're talking about."

"And if you lose it, you might get canned, huh baby?"

"I told you. I don't know what you're—"

"Women are such shitty liars."

He dropped his laundry bag of cash and grabbed at the purse, jerking it from her and looked inside. What the hell—nothing but folded paper bags. He dumped them out; they scattered on the floor. A note fell out too. He bent down and read it—

PUT ONE THOUSAND DOLLARS
IN THIS BAG
OR ELSE

then looked up into the muzzle of a .38. He had that I-don't-believe-this-shit-is-happening expression when Lona pulled the trigger, sending a slug crashing into his knee. His gun fell and clattered.

Dan jumped up and grabbed it.

"Damn you," the Texan said, hugging his knee and almost crying. "Damn you, damn you, damn you!"

"Thou shalt not steal," Lona said as she grabbed her purse.

"Come on," Dan said, snatching up the laundry bag of cash.

Even as sirens wailed in the distance, they were out the door with a bag filled with four hundred dollars, according to the news, but seventy-four thousand in reality. The teller had not followed procedure (filling the bag with small denominations), nor had she put in one of those still-experimental exploding packets that would splatter every bill in the bag with ink, because those were in the cash drawer, not on the cart. Some of that would come out in the paper the next day. The bank president was quoted as saying that the cowardly robbers were lucky to get four hundred, and lucky the security guard had a stroke after shooting down one of the scoundrels.

WHILE DAN WAS OUT getting Lona her breakfast biscuits, Lona read the news story again and laughed, for she took this to be a sign that she was destined to live in Louisiana with Dan, Jesus providing the seed money to get them started on a life together. Maybe they'd even get married!

$74,150—they'd counted it before putting it back in the bag, and the bag back in the trunk of the car. Sure, she'd stuck one bundle of twenties in her purse, but Dan had seen this and demanded it back. He didn't want to "dissipate" their nest egg, he said. But she said don't be stupid, the whole point was dissipating it, and he finally gave in. Now she threw herself on the motel bed and whooped, without a care that somebody might hear her. They were wealthy now, and wealth granted you immunity, didn't it? You could yell as loud as you wanted if you were rich enough. You could do anything.

It did bother her a bit that the paper said they were armed and dangerous. It bothered her even more that the artist's sketch of the stick-up couple showed a childishly drawn woman with short hair and a perfectly rendered splotch on her neck—a birthmark that looked, as one witness had said, like a leech.

"You couldn't help but stare at it," the paper quoted him, "and think she'd been marked by the devil."

"So what if I have freckles," Lona said to herself.

Still, she grabbed her purse and went into the bathroom. Her birthmark seemed darker and larger than ever. She rubbed it with a washcloth until the skin turned red. Then she got out her Max Factor and began sponging it on. Not too bad, she thought, twisting her head to get a look. Kind of like a burn scar. She was still studying it when she heard the siren. It's nothing, she told herself. Just some speeder on the highway.

Just some car chase on Airline Highway.

But the siren kept getting louder.

16

So where do you keep pigs?

Jute and me debated that question and we decided to dig a hole for them. That's what I told Pawpaw when he saw us taking spoons from the kitchen drawer.

"Well," he said, "guess I can buy new spoons."

"We won't hurt them."

"Uh-huh." He lit a cigar and looked out the window. I guess he was feeling kinda poor after buying two cases of Mason jars. You'd think Memaw would have forgiven him, since she got all new jars, but she didn't.

Pawpaw used to plant his field in Indian corn and watermelons, but he'd stopped two years before. He said the government paid him not to grow rice, and I said you already don't grow rice, and he said yeah, so it was a good deal all around. I wondered if the government would pay me not to learn, but I expected not.

I let Jute pick out the poke for the pigs, for *his* pigs anyway, since they were small ones, Billy Bob and Willy Nilly.

"Bee Bee and Billy Bog," he corrected me.

He picked out a spot on top a small hill that was mostly made of Lunch Time's poop, and I pointed out that would only increase the amount of digging we'd have to do. Better if we got a head start by digging in a low area. He thought about that and finally said all right, we could try that, but he wasn't going to dig in rocks. And I said the only rocks were on the road. He wanted to know why, and I said rocks just naturally migrated to where there were cars. Uncle Dan taught me that. I hardly needed to go to school with all the stuff he was teaching me.

Jute and me sat facing each other and began to dig in dirt as black and loamy as old coffee grounds. We each had a Mason jar—which we were under threat of death if we broke—Jute's with root beer and mine with red drink. I did most of the digging and Jute did most of the drinking. Pretty soon he needed to pee, but he was so dirty I told him to go in the field and pee. He looked around.

"I can't pee in the field."

"Why not? You pee in the bed."

He thought about that and finally walked off to pee in some tall grass. It might've been a coincidence, but right then the little hole I'd dug began to fill up with water. I imagined it was yellow, and I was afraid it might be pee, but Mrs. Bertrand said I had an overactive brain and nerves pulled too tight, and she was right. So much was going on, I had a hard time keeping track of it all.

The water was now coming over the rim of the hole, like when the drain of the bathtub stopped up with our boats. I picked up the Mason jars and retreated. Jute came over and looked at it.

"What's all that water?" he said.

"I don't know, exactly."

"Uh oh."

"What?"

"You broke it."

"You're crazy. I didn't break anything."

"You broke the ground."

"I didn't break the ground!"

"Did too."

"Didn't. And anyway, the ground's not something you can break."

"You gonna get whipped, Charlie."

I sighed. Maybe Jute was right. The world didn't make any sense, so why shouldn't I get whipped for breaking it?

We made the best of this development by getting our plastic Civil War soldiers and staging the battle of New Orleans. That wasn't much of a battle, not in reality, but reality didn't matter to us much. In our game the rebs won every time, mostly because Jute always took the Union side, and he didn't know what he was doing. Like when all his blue men drowned in the rising water before he noticed. He started crying, and I had to help him get them out, but of course that meant they were captured and had to carry General Lee on their backs and shine his boots. And Jute had to get me a red drink to release them.

The water kept rising. We had to retreat to the rim of the hollow before it finally stopped, having made a lake about thirty feet wide. Could we keep our pigs in there, Jute wanted to know.

"I don't think so," I told him, "but they can drink out of it."

Jute blinked. "They can drink out of the ground?"

"Sure."

He seemed impressed with this idea, and as he was thirsty anyway, he knelt down and lapped water like a dog because nobody'd taught him how to cup his hands, not that he could've anyway, since he was holding his empty Mason jar.

He looked up. "It's salty."

I knew then that this water was one of two things—either water from the Gulf of Mexico that had somehow leaked under Pawpaw's farm, or it was pee.

Lunch Time had wandered over and now noticed the water. She stuck her tongue in it, looked up at us and shook her mane. Then she went back to drinking. It might've been nasty ole pee or seawater, but at least somebody liked it.

17

Dan

DAN HAD BOUGHT four pounds of boudin with the other groceries, and he was now nibbling on the spicy sausage as he drove back to the Pontchartrain Motel in Kenner. The radio was playing Elvis and he was singing along. The trouble with Elvis was that Dan always drove faster while listening to the King, like a hundred sometimes, and that was probably why the cop pulled out behind him. He considered not punching it for just a moment, but of course he did. A white backfire of smoke swirled in the rearview, and with some deft swerving in traffic, he soon left the law far behind.

"Don't mess with the King, boys," he said.

At the next bend in the road he made a squealing right onto a side street, then rumbled through a parking lot to watch the fuzz zoom by, siren and lights going. Then he got back on the main road, slow and legal, and continued on to the Pontchartrain, chomping on boudin and occasionally sipping a Coke. He'd just turned off the engine in the parking lot when that cop car slammed into the curb, barreled across the short stretch of grass and almost hit his front fender. The cop's siren died, and Dan's Coke fell to the floorboard.

"This ain't good," he said.

Two cops jumped out with their guns drawn. Cursing Elvis and his boudin habit, Dan threw up his hands. Glancing at the motel he saw Lona in a doorway in a towel, then she was gone. He wondered if that would be the last time he saw her.

"What the devil do you think you're doing?"

Dan looked up at the cop in his window—a short man with a black mustache. His khaki uniform was neatly pressed and the pelican on his badge was mirror bright. "Puttin' up my hands?" Dan said.

The cop shook his head with a trace of amusement. "You're a wise fellow, aren't you lad? So what's your name?"

"Joe. Joe Bazooka."

"Ah, a brilliant alias." He pulled open Dan's door. "I want you to get out now with your hands where I can see them. And if you try to run I'll shoot you down. Do you understand?"

"Loud and clear, officer."

The other cop holstered his gun and opened the back door of the Roadmaster. He dug in the bag of groceries and pulled out the remainder of Dan's boudin. The sausage was as long as the cop was tall. "Where'd you get this, boy?"

"Winn Dixie." Dan was standing away from the car with his hands half up.

"Hell, that ain't no good. Chain stores ain't no good." He dropped it on the pavement.

"Hey man, that's—"

"Best you keep quiet," the mustached cop said. "He's saving you from a case of botulism." He reached around the steering wheel and grabbed the keys. "Do you have anything in the trunk?"

"I do if you got a warrant."

"We don't need a warrant. You're already a fugitive, running from a blue light. Driving erratically, suspicion of drunkenness. And what do you have in that Coke can, may I ask?"

"I got Coke in that Coke can, you dumbass," Dan said, unable to stop the devil inside him from having its say.

The cop chuckled and holstered his own gun. "Harry, did you hear this cretin?"

"Sure did, Clint."

"That's insulting an officer of the law, not to mention public use of inflammatory language. What else, Harry?"

"I dunno," Harry said. "Is the dumbass drunk?"

"I'll ask him. Are you inebriated, sir?"

"If that means drunk, I wish I was."

"Oh that's lovely! Tell the judge that and you'll never get out."

Clint walked around to the trunk, stuck the key in and popped it. In there was a cardboard box with women's clothes spilling out, and a laundry bag. He yanked on the bag. "What's in here?"

"The wife's dirty panties. Whaja think?"

Clint let it go in disgust. He had his hand on the trunk, ready to close it when he noticed the suspect acting overly nonchalant, and that made him interested again. He pulled the bag up by its cinch string and looked inside.

"Well, well." He glanced at Dan and called out, "You may be

the most astounding cretin I've ever met." As Dan didn't reply, Clint left it there and came around to stand in Dan's face. "Time to truss him up," he said to his partner.

"You bet." When Dan suddenly tried to run, Harry tripped him, kneed him in the back, then clapped on the cuffs. "Resisting arrest. Attempted escape. Keep it up, boy, you're doing good."

"We have a major scofflaw here, Harry. He's not just an ordinary cretin. He's a bank robber and a homicide enthusiast."

"Murderer," Harry said happily.

"I didn't murder anybody," Dan said into the asphalt.

"You remember that guard you shot? He expired this morning. And your buddy you kneecapped, he's talking a blue streak."

"The guard was already dead, and that cowboy is the bank robber, not me."

"How marvelous! Did you hear his confession, Harry?"

"Yep. The dumb shit admits to being there." Harry jerked his prisoner up, then half led, half dragged him to their car and shoved him onto the backseat. Harry slammed the door and went back to his partner. "How'd you know it's him?"

"Let me put it this way. From what I found in his trunk, it's him without a doubt. And I'll tell you something else. If we handle this right, we'll be living like kings."

They talked a bit more, then went through Dan's car a second time, finding a Bible under the front seat, then Dan's gun and a box of bullets in the glove compartment. Along with a registration certificate from Missouri saying the car belonged to the Tijuana Bible Company.

"Tijuana Bible Company?" Clint said.

"They make those fuck books," Harry said.

"Is that a fact?"

"Yep. And sell 'em to Catholic schoolchildren." He flipped through the Bible he'd found under the seat and held it out, open to the story of Solomon.

"That's appalling," Clint said.

"I had one like this. We all did. I learned a lot more from the Book of Kings than from any of those nuns, tell you that."

Clint took the Bible and turned a page. Then another one. "Filth, and in a Bible no less."

"Come on. Don't be such a prude."

"I'm not a prude." Clint tossed the book back to Harry, walked around, grabbed the laundry bag from the trunk and stuffed it into the trunk of his own car.

"You can't do this," Dan said as Clint got in behind the wheel.

"I can't do what?" Clint said, meticulously wiping his hands on a handkerchief.

"Arrest me like this, without proper cause."

"You've been in the system before, I see."

"Hey, I just know my rights, like any American."

"You lost those rights when I found your loot."

"That's my grandfather's money. He willed it to me."

"What a wonderful story! A whole estate stuffed in a laundry bag."

"That's how he kept it. He didn't believe in banks."

"How unfortunate for you, then, that he used those bank wrappers stamped with 'Southern Bank of Baton Rouge.'"

Dan bit his lip. "Hey come on. How 'bout I make a donation?"

Clint laughed. "Forget it, Mr. Bazooka. We're like those G men. Untouchable and incorruptible."

"And that's attempted bribery," Harry added as he slid into the passenger side of the front seat. "I'm keeping track of all your crimes, ass-brain." He pulled out a pen, clicked it and started writing.

Dan sat back, vowing never to listen to Lona, or any woman, ever again. Like bank robbery was a good idea! It wouldn't take more than a week for his fingerprints to pop with the FBI, and then these cops would discover he'd escaped from prison in Missouri. And in Alaska. And that his picture was up in post offices in probably half a dozen states. Then put bank robbery on top of all that. Jeez. He'd be sitting in Angola with Landry before long. At least Landry had lived it up for a while, with all his girls.

Dan thought of the laundry bag of money in the trunk of this patrol car, and the only thing he'd bought with it were a few groceries, some boudin, Cokes, pretzels, and…damn! He'd forgotten Lona's biscuits! Man, she'd be so disappointed. He shook his head. If he got out of this, first thing he'd do, he'd get her those biscuits. This wasn't her fault, anyway. It was his. Driving too fast to "Blue Moon." Who does that with the proceeds from a robbery in the trunk? Devil Dan was a dumbass like they said, he really was.

They were just pulling out the lot when a second patrol car showed up, making a less dramatic entrance than the first.

"Party crashers," Clint observed.

The new car drove slowly around the backside of the Roadmaster and Dan noticed that one of them was on the radio, probably calling in the license plate—which would be reported as stolen in no time. Dan looked out at the six feet of boudin now cooking on the hot pavement and thought, what a waste.

18

Lunch Time was gone. As Jute and me walked the pasture, I kept thinking we'd come across her body. She was pretty old, and Memaw said if Lunch Time died, that was it, no more horses. Jute was sniveling; I told him to stop, but a minute later he started again. We'd about walked the whole field when I saw Pawpaw come out the house. He walked straight over to the lake we'd made and stood over it. Then squatted down and studied it for a while, and I could feel a sharp tingling in my butt.

This was not good.

"Charlie!" he yelled. "Git over here."

No, this was not good at all.

I went running in his direction. I kept expecting to hear Jute saying how I was gonna get whipped, but he didn't say it this time. Or maybe he did and I didn't hear him. When I looked back he was far behind, looking around like Lunch Time might've been standing right behind him all along.

"Did you see this?" Pawpaw said when I got to him.

"Uh-huh," I said. "Did you make that for Lunch Time?" Those words just popped out, and while I was used to lying to get out of trouble, this question seemed awfully smart. It was beyond smart and I would remember it for ever and ever.

If it had worked, that is.

"Don't pull that on me, Charlie. I saw y'all digging in here."

"Just with some spoons."

"Just with those soup spoons you took out the drawer?"

"Uh-huh."

"And where are they now, Charlie?"

"What?"

"The spoons, where are they? Lidia is fit to be tied. She counts them every day and she's a couple short."

"Oh, ah, I dunno."

"You don't know?"

"I might've left them in the hole."

He just looked at me and sighed. Jute came up then. He wasn't crying, but his eyes were the color of bubblegum.

"Now I have to buy your memaw new spoons. Or I suppose you could get them."

"I could?" Was he saying I had to buy new spoons?

"You remember about where you left them?"

"Oh yeah." I pointed. "Right there in the middle."

"You think you could find them?"

"Sure, I can find them."

"All right. Let's see if you can. But don't drown, 'cause I'm not going in after you."

"No sir, I won't." And I wouldn't, as the pool couldn't be more than six inches deep, though I knew that Pawpaw wasn't fooling when he said he wouldn't come after me. I knew he couldn't swim that well.

I rolled up my jeans, took one step into the water, and felt how cold it was, like ice water. "It's cold," I said.

"It's cold," Jute echoed, and I saw him shiver.

I took another step and went down to my knees. This was deeper than I thought—the patches on my jeans were getting wet. Another step and my foot kept going down. I went underwater and remembered to hold my nose, because if you let water in your nose, you drown. I looked up and saw the sun glittering through dirty water. Then I looked down, and if the pool had a bottom, I couldn't see it. I kicked twice and broke the surface.

"Jesus Christ," Pawpaw said.

Jute was bawling.

I clawed onto an underwater ledge and crawled through the shallow part. Pawpaw leaned over and pulled me up. "You okay?"

I licked my lips and tasted the salt. "Uh-huh, I guess."

Pawpaw stared at the hole for a solid minute, then he said, "You know what this is, Charlie?"

"A hole in the ground?"

"It's a lot more than that. It's an honest-to-God fact of nature."

Pawpaw forgot about the spoons, and he spent most of the day trying to survey this fact of nature that had miraculously appeared on his property. First he used a pole, but as it wouldn't touch bottom, he got a rope and tied knots in it, then tied one end to the sprocket I'd used as an anvil. He tossed the sprocket in the water and played it out till it got slack, with me counting the knots as he pulled it up.

"How many was that, Charlie?" he said.

"Twelve knots."

"They're fathoms."

"Okay."

"Write it down."

He spelled it for me. I wrote it on my Big Chief tablet and put "12" underneath. Pawpaw moved a few feet over and threw the sprocket again. We went all the way round, and before long I had a column of numbers that went on for three pages. I'm not sure what they meant, but the biggest one was sixteen. Most of them were sixteen because that's all the rope Pawpaw had. He said he needed to get a longer rope to find the bottom.

"Maybe there ain't one," I said.

"Ain't what?"

"A bottom."

He dropped the rope like he was ready for a break, but actually he was thinking. "I've always thought the earth was like a coconut," he said finally. "All husk with juice inside."

"A coconut you get from the store?"

"Yeah Charlie, so you might be right about the bottom."

"I am?"

"There might not be one."

19

Dan

TWO COPS EASED OUT of the car parked behind the Roadmaster. One sauntered around each side, looking in the windows before coming over to Clint and Harry's car.

"Sandy, Bert," Clint said, glancing from one window to the other. "How are you lads today?"

"Oh not too bad," Sandy said. "Who you got back there? Wouldn't be that speed demon, would it?"

"This here's Joe Bazooka in the flesh," Harry said. "Caught him flying a hundred miles an hour down Airline Highway."

Sandy bent down and studied Dan in the backseat. "Hey Joe," he said. He rapped on the glass, but the prisoner just stared straight ahead. "Unfriendly cuss."

"Maybe because he has a disability," Clint said.

"He's deaf, is he?"

"Oh I don't know about deaf. But he does have a lead foot…and marmalade for brains."

Sandy shaded the glass with his hand. "He looks familiar."

"Perhaps you've arrested him before?"

"Could be. You want us to get his car towed?"

"Already taken care of."

"Okay then." Sandy patted the rooftop.

"Be seeing you," Clint said as they began to roll.

BERT CAME OVER to his partner. "Something wrong?"

Sandy shook his head. "I dunno. But he sure does look familiar."

"Joe Bazooka ain't a real name. It's like that bubblegum. The one with the comic strip."

Sandy rubbed his bottom lip. "I've seen a picture of that boy somewhere. And not on a comic strip."

OFFICER CLINT HAD DRIVEN so far out of town that Dan was beginning to get worried. They were off the main road, and now the road turned to gravel, and gravel soon gave way to oiled-down dirt.

"You lost?" Dan asked.

"Shut up," Harry said. "He knows where he's going."

Cops were never fun people, but Dan found Harry to be more unpleasant than necessary. And he knew that seventy thousand dollars was a hell of a temptation. They might even kill him for it, to keep him from talking. This suspicion took on a sickening reality when Clint cut the car onto a narrow lane between rotting cypresses dripping with moss. He thought of Charlie and

Jute, and how they needed him. He couldn't die now; it wouldn't be right.

A bit of fishtailing through a mucky stretch, and they finally pulled up to a cabin constructed half of logs, unpainted and gray with age. The chinking was gone, the roof sagging and caved in on one side. All around, tall weeds flickered with sunlight.

"This where you live, Harry?" Dan asked, fighting back a growing nausea. "'Cause if you need some cash to brighten things up—"

"Why don't you shut your trap?" Harry snapped.

Clint made a U in the weeds and pointed the car back to the narrow road. Killed the engine.

With his hands cuffed behind his back, Dan had fallen over in the seat. His head was spinning, and the sudden stop in this desolate place hadn't helped any. "I'm sick," he said. "I gotta throw up."

"What a liar," Harry said.

"Possibly," Clint said, "but I don't relish the aroma of regurgitated boudin in the car."

Harry cursed, got out, opened the back door and yanked Dan by the collar. Dan slid out the door and fell head-first to the ground. Then threw up. "The dumbass wasn't lying."

"Seems he has a feeble stomach to go with his even feebler intellect." Clint was out of the car now, holding a silver derringer with a mother-of-pearl handle—a lady's .22.

"I like that," Harry said.

"Thank you. How about you, Joe? Are you an aficionado of pistols?"

"I guess," Dan said, still spitting.

"Excellent." Clint polished the gun on his sleeve and admired the mirror finish. "I bought this the other day at a quaint shop on Magazine Street. They take cash and don't ask any questions."

"Yeah? And why should I care?"

"I think you would, because I'm going to call it Joe Bazooka."

"Bazooka," Harry said, laughing. "Little gun like that."

Dan suddenly tried to get up. Harry kicked him with a boot to the ribs. Dan rolled over on his back.

"Yes indeed," Clint went on. "I'm going to name it after that cop killer we have in New Orleans. Only nobody's ever heard of him. Not yet, anyway."

"I'm not one for history," Dan confessed.

"No, I suppose not." Clint flicked open the cylinder and spun it, then closed it. "Tell me, Joe. Are you a religious man?"

"You sure ask a lot of questions."

"I'm only trying to be sociable."

Dan shut his eyes against the sun. "All right then. Yeah, but I ain't been to church lately."

"How about you, Harry?"

"Oh hell no. If I learned anything in St. Vincent's, religion is a bunch of crap."

"Is that right? Then where do you go when you're dead?"

"When you're dead you're dead. There ain't nothin' else."

"I have to say, Harry, that's a terrible outlook."

"You got a better one?"

"How about this?" Clint lifted the pistol and shot Harry in the forehead. Harry grunted and went down.

"Jesus Christ!" Dan said.

"Precisely." Clint squatted next to Harry, gingerly took his jaw and twisted his head from side to side. No resistance. "Rest in peace, my lad." He pulled Harry's pistol from his holster and turned to Dan. "I had enough of him, if you want the truth."

"Yeah, so you just kill him like that?"

Clint shrugged. "He had a tongue on him. He would have ruined everything."

"And what about me?"

"I've asked myself that question for the last half hour. And I confess that you're growing on me, Joe. You might even prove to be useful."

"Hey, I'm game if you are, but what about your pal here? How you gonna explain that hole in his head?"

"Oh, that shouldn't be too difficult. Let's see…what if I say you confessed to hiding out here, so we investigated, and lo, found a whole nest of bank robbers. A wild shootout ensued, and Harry was struck down and killed by an accomplice of the notorious villain, Joe Bazooka."

"You say that, you gotta give it up."

"Give up what?"

"The money."

"Oh, a bit, perhaps. Suppose I salt a few bills here and there and say the bank robbers must have buried the rest. They'll be digging for weeks before they decide one of their own found it and stole it. Many in law enforcement are criminals, sad to say."

"That's a stupid plan."

"Is it now? And how do you conclude that?"

"'Cause of that car coming up."

"There isn't—"

But there was. The sound was unmistakable now—the whirr of an engine, tires squishing through mud. "Damn," Clint said under his breath. He looked around, tossed Harry's gun next to him, grabbed Dan by the shirt and lifted him up, then pushed him toward the cabin at gunpoint. "The fact is, I'm starting to like you, Joe. I don't want to have to kill you. So stay down and keep quiet, and we'll split the money, okay?"

"Okay," Dan said, even though he knew Clint was lying about everything he'd just said.

The inside of the cabin was actually worse than the outside. Floorboards had rotted away and Dan saw sloshing water, murky with life. Out the glassless back window was a cypress swamp. Clint forced Dan to the floor, uncuffed one of his hands, slipped the chain around a floorboard, and recuffed him.

OF ALL THE CARS that might've shown up, this was the worst. With a single whoop of its siren, the other cop car from the Pontchartrain Motel tore around the corner, then slid to a stop about fifty feet away. Both cops jumped out with guns drawn, then put them away and ran to Clint, who was leaning over his partner.

20

W E W E R E A L L I N T H E K I T C H E N when Memaw showed up in the Ford. She didn't say anything, just went on back to her bedroom and slammed the door.

"Lidia?" Pawpaw said, but she didn't answer.

I figured she had the red ass on account of the spoons, but Pawpaw said don't worry about the spoons; she blamed him, not me. I didn't like Pawpaw getting blamed for something I did, so I said let's blame it on Jute 'cause Jute never gets blamed for anything. Jute said "uh-uh," and Pawpaw said that was un-Christian and I was too much like his own boys. If I had a mother things would be different.

"I had a mother," I said.

"You sure did."

"Did I have a mother?" Jute asked.

"Both you boys had a mother, but she blew away in a hurricane."

"Is she coming back?" Jute said.

"No. She's with Jesus now."

I thought about this, then I said, "How would things be different? Would I still be a bastard?"

Pawpaw looked up. "Don't say that word."

"Mousey Bertrand said I was a bastard."

"Mousey Bertrand don't know a thing. You're not one of those, and I want you to forget that word, you hear me?"

"Yes sir."

"Christian folks don't say such things."

"Are we Christian?"

"Of course we're Christian! Don't you go to church every Sunday?"

"Yeah, but I thought I was Catholic."

"That's Christian too, just the best kind of Christian."

"Oh."

"So what'd you think it meant?"

"What?"

"Being a Christian."

I shrugged. "Presents on Christmas?"

"Presents," Jute agreed.

"It means you're going to heaven. Lots of others don't go to heaven, because they're not Christian."

"Oh."

"And you'll see your mama in heaven."

"I will?"

"If you pray really hard and don't kill anybody."

I thought of what Memaw had said, that Jesus would understand. "If I pray really hard, will Mama come back?"

"No Charlie, once you're dead you stay dead."

"Always?"

"Uh-huh."

"Is Lunch Time dead?" Jute asked.

"I don't know," Pawpaw said. "Looks like she got loose somehow."

Memaw came in then, noisily washed her gun in the sink (even though it wasn't Sunday) and hung it on a nail to dry. Then she clattered pots and pans and referred to Pawpaw as Gussie, which was her way of driving us out the kitchen when she wasn't happy about something. It was pretty effective.

21

Dan

DAN WATCHED THROUGH A GAP in the boards as the three cops knelt around their fallen buddy. One felt for a pulse, then they stood. One cop pointed at the cabin, but Clint shook his head and pointed to an oak near the edge of the swamp. That side of the cabin had fallen away, and Dan saw a path behind that old tree that led through the thicket of cypress. Before long he saw all three cops jogging through there, two of them with shotguns. One of the new cops was in the lead. When he turned and glanced at the house, Dan flattened down and prayed that the shadows were black enough to hide him.

Now they were gone and Dan put his mind to getting out of those handcuffs. Fortunately, he'd studied with quite a few experts in the field of escaping from justice. His teachers claimed to know what worked in desperate circumstances, though the fact they were securely in prison should have given him pause.

Dan unbuckled the watch Lona had given him and slipped the tongue of the buckle into the keyhole and lifted up—the recommended technique. Then he pushed down, then sideways. Nothing. He repeated that with random variations. Minutes of struggling that did nothing but accidently make the cuffs tighter. Frustrated, he yanked on the board and it crumbled into bits. God, what luck! Except now his watch slipped from his hands and fell into the muck. And when he got to his knees, more boards gave way and his legs crashed through. Hanging now by his elbows, his feet felt cold and wet, live bait in swamp water he figured was thrashing with alligators and water moccasins. He jerked up, tearing his pants in the process. The fabric was dotted now with blood. Worse, he heard shots—two pops in rapid succession. The sun was going down, and Clint was no doubt saving a third pop, just for Joe Bazooka.

22

I WONDERED IF UNCLE DAN and Aunt Lona were selling their books, and how boring that must be compared to discovering facts of nature like we had. I thought of what Pawpaw had said about living on a coconut, and soon as I put my head down for our afternoon nap, I dreamed the earth was a coconut on a coconut tree and fell off in a storm. It landed on a glowing rock and broke open, and all the people on it—who swarmed over it like lice—jumped off and burned up on the rock. Jute—who'd woken me up—had a dream too. He dreamt he was swimming in an ocean of pee, and Pawpaw told him he could pee all he wanted in the ocean, 'cause the ocean was pee anyway. So he did.

His wasn't all a dream—I could tell by the smell.

Dan

THINKING IT MIGHT COME in handy, Dan grabbed Harry's badge, ripping it from his shirt. He glanced at the name—Harry Belemi—then ran around to the driver's side of Clint's car and jumped in, reaching for the key. Wasn't there, damn it. He slid under the dashboard and stared at far more wires than he'd ever seen before under a dash, probably because this was a cop car and therefore highly accessorized. Taking an educated guess, he pulled out two of the four red wires and twisted them together. Then he pulled out the brown wire and touched it to the bare copper of the red wires. The siren began whining.

Shit.

Nothing he'd learned in prison was working out.

When he looked up, a hole appeared in the windshield, right above his head, then another one. Through the fractures he saw Clint in the distance, pointing with a pistol. Dan ducked just as more bullets splattered the glass. He grabbed a handful of wires below the dash and jerked them loose with both hands, smashed the radio mike against the steering column, then rolled out the door and ran for the other cruiser. Fortunately, his way was shielded by a stand of palmettos, but that didn't stop Clint from firing blindly through them. A bullet plugged a fallen branch and set it spinning. Dan jumped over it, yelling for dumbass Clint to keep on shooting, he might get lucky.

This produced a flurry of shots followed by incoherent yelling, then all went quiet. Clint was probably reloading. Too bad for him, as Sandy and Bert had left the key in the ignition and soon Dan was hauling down that dirt road. Without the money, though, which was a major pisser.

USING A PAPERCLIP he found by dumping everything from the glove compartment, Dan freed himself from the cuffs and tossed them out the window. Within forty five minutes he was rolling down U.S. 90 at more than a hundred miles an hour. He was using the lights, but not the siren. He'd also turned off the 2-way. It amused him to see drivers' reactions to a cop car bearing down on their bumpers. A Volkswagen full of teenagers ran off road and into a drainage ditch, where it tilted precariously on two wheels before gently rolling over.

"Drive careful!" he yelled out his window.

Miles went by, then the flashing lights of a cop car far ahead. They'd pulled somebody for speeding, most likely. As he flew by, he saw the car they'd stopped—a Buick Roadmaster very much like his own car. And standing in front of it, gesticulating at a pair of cops, was a woman who looked very much like his own woman.

Dan hit the brakes and almost lost control getting his car over to the parking lane, then threw it into reverse. He stomped on the gas before squealing to a stop, forcing those cops to jump out of the way. He reached into his shirt pocket for Harry's badge, but the clip had broken off. Crap, he shouldn't have yanked it like that. Noticing a piece of chewed gum either Sandy or Bert had left in a coffee cup, he popped it in his mouth and chomped it a couple of times to soften it, then used it to stick the badge to his shirt. He hoped it'd stick long enough.

An off-duty cop in street clothes with a badge stuck on with bubblegum? Why the hell not?

He got out and headed toward them, letting every memory of cops flood through his mind—and he had quite a few, most of them unpleasant. Cops were generally morons, he told himself, so how difficult could this be?

"Got a report," he said, almost winking at Lona, who he figured was doing her best not to throw her arms around him, "of a lady manhandled by a couple of redneck morons. Claimed it was police brutality."

"That's a frigging lie," snapped one of the cops.

The other one looked back at his own cruiser. "What woman did they mean?"

"You manhandling more than one?"

"That's none of your beeswax," he said. "Just who the devil are you, anyway?"

"Harry Belafonte. Call the captain if you want."

"I might just do that."

"Suit yourself. Now, little lady, you got a problem with these guys?"

"I—"

"Hey! You can't talk to her!"

"Why not?"

"Because she's ours. We caught her and she's frigging ours."

"She must be a pretty big fish."

"Bank robber," said the other one, who now had Lona's arm. "Found the loot on her. Some of it."

"Is that right? Hey, not that deal in Baton Rouge? What was it? Southern Bank or something?"

"Yep," he said, and Dan thought if he puffed up any more he'd bust his buttons.

"I heard they only got four hundred."

"You heard wrong. They got a whole lot more than four hundred."

"Like what?"

"Can't tell you that," the other cop said.

"It's some big secret, huh?"

"Like I said, it's confidential."

"Uh-huh. Well, you guys sure gonna look foolish when you show up with the wrong girl."

Traffic had died on the highway, and now they were in a real Louisiana darkness, just the revolving lights of the cruisers sweeping the area like two helicopters. The cops looked at each other. "She had some of the money," one said.

"You check the serial numbers? And where's that fingerprint of Satan she's supposed to have?"

The cop fumbled with his flashlight and flashed it over Lona's neck. Not seeing the mark, he went around with the light while she put up one hand against the glare. "Goddammit, he's right."

"Like I said before, you guys are morons."

The cop turned and shone his light into Harry's face, then

down his body. "We're morons, huh? So what happened to your pants?"

Harry looked down at his ripped, mud-smeared and blood-soaked khakis. "Well, I'll be. Will yah look at that."

The cop now put one hand on his belt, his fingertips brushing his gun. "Who you with again?"

"I already said—"

"Wait, wait a sec." The cop with Lona turned his head at the creak of a car door. "You hear that?"

"Jee-sus," the other cop said. He took off for his cruiser and jogged around the back bumper, then shouted, "She's running."

"Lost somebody?" Dan shouted as the cop ran off toward the bordering woods. The cop was chasing someone, the two figures flickering like will-o'-wisps in the dark.

The cop with Lona watched this with alarm. He suddenly jerked Lona's arm and pushed her toward Dan. "Take her, Harry. She's yours."

"What if I don't want her?" Dan said, and Lona gave him a furious look.

"Hey, make yourself useful. We got an emergency." He now hauled after the first cop who was already into the woods, shinning his flashlight wildly. A shot. Then another one.

Lona ran over to Dan. He was about to suggest she not act all lovey dovey when she hauled off and slapped him. He heard a clink but didn't notice his badge had fallen off. "What the hell was that for?" he said.

"That was for leaving me and taking all the money."

"But I—"

"And not bringing my biscuits."

"Listen, Lona, we can't be having an argument here. They'll be coming back." Traffic was picking up too, and Dan was buffeted by the big trucks. The air had turned cool; drizzle sparkled in the flash of headlights.

"You can just go on in your cop car. I'm taking the Roadster."

"They got an APB on it. Why do you think you were stopped?"

She looked at the Roadmaster uncertainly, then back at Dan. "Oh, I don't know. I just need to get my stuff." She ran back to the Roadmaster and got her purse, then returned to Dan, then ran back yet again to get her clothes from the back.

"Lona, Jesus! You're acting like a chicken with its head cut off."

"You're the one with its head cut off." Finally she ran by him saying, "Come on. Don't just stand there."

He shook his head, wondering how he'd ever considered marrying her. What a mistake that would be! She'd drive him stir crazy in a week.

THEY WERE ABOUT TEN MILES down the road, arguing about Dan's insensitivity, which was notorious in Lona's opinion. Did he have to mention her freckle? Couldn't he think of anything better to tell them? Why? Why the fuck did he have to tell them that?

Apparently, the mere mention of her birthmark implied the most horrible and critical thoughts about it, and Dan was on the defensive until he finally managed to turn her attention to a more immediately compelling subject—to Harry and Clint and how they stole the—

"You lost the money!"

"They *stole* it. I was lucky to get out with my skin."

"Your skin ain't worth that much." She pummeled the glove

compartment with her fists, then pushed back in the seat, arms crossed over her chest. After some silent fuming, she looked back at him as the cabin flashed with lights from the oncoming traffic.

"I tore my pants," Dan admitted.

"What do I care?"

"I think you would. You bought them."

She looked him over more carefully now. "Where's the watch?"

"What watch?"

"The *watch*. The watch I gave you."

"Ahhh—"

"I had it inscribed and everything."

He just shrugged.

"Oh Dan, how could you?"

"He's an inconsiderate asshole if you ask me," said a woman's voice from behind them. Lona screamed, and when Dan turned to look at the handcuffed stowaway lying on the backseat, he accidentally stomped on the gas, rear-ending a double-decker chicken truck.

24

THE WATER WAS COMING OVER the top of the hole, so Pawpaw had his John Deere tractor out and was building a levee around it with a dozer blade, pushing dirt up against what he was now calling "Charlie's Hole." I didn't feel all that good about the name, since it had eaten Memaw's spoons and was now threatening to flood Pawpaw's field—not that the field was good for anything anymore now that Lunch Time was gone and the government was paying Pawpaw not to plant anything on it. I told Pawpaw we could call it "Jute's Pee Hole" and he said that was a good name, but Jute probably wouldn't like it. And if Memaw heard it, I might get a whipping.

Between what Jute wouldn't like and Memaw wouldn't like, there wasn't much left.

Pawpaw spent half the morning building that levee, and he was almost done when a car came tearing up our driveway. A police car. It pulled up in front of the house in a cloud of dust, and when the dust drifted off we saw the sheriff standing there, looking at us.

IF YOU WANTED TO COOK UP a sheriff for Vermilion Parish from scratch, you'd first need a saddle you'd left in the rain, some cracked aggies for eyes, and a straw cowboy hat. Then you'd simmer him on our one-thousand-watt radio station and stuff his shirt pocket with five dollar bills. That last part was for buying him votes, according to Pawpaw. The sheriff wasn't such a good guy, but if not for him my daddy would've got twenty-five years instead of just fifteen. He might've got life. He'd done a lot more than the state knew about.

The sheriff and Pawpaw were now standing on the levee Pawpaw had almost finished, their boots sinking in the soft dirt. Pawpaw was telling the Sheriff how Charlie's Hole was a fact of nature.

The sheriff scratched his old-saddle chin and said, "You might be right. I've never seen anything like it except for those sink holes they have in limestone country. But we don't have any limestone around here. Mud, sand and clay for thousands of feet."

"That right?"

"I'm no geologist, but I'd talk to one if I were you."

"Sounds like that'd cost a lotta money."

"There's a professor in Lafayette who's not exactly a geologist, but he likes to investigate stuff for a book he's working on. The 'Mountain of Louisiana,' he calls it."

"What mountain is that?"

"He says there was one not far from here, millions of years

ago." The sheriff wrote something on his note pad, tore off the page, and handed it to Pawpaw.

Pawpaw folded it, stuck it in his pocket, then turned back to the hole. "It's not just the water, but it's salt water. I'd like to know how salt water could be bubbling up miles from the coast."

"Lot of strange stuff going on."

"Uh-huh. Like what?"

"Like Maurice Leduc getting shot."

"I know a Leduc. Lolly Leduc."

"Maurice got himself shot yesterday morning. Apparently he heard somebody fussing, came out his bath naked with a rifle, took one in the chest. Killed him like that." The sheriff snapped his fingers.

"Sorry to hear it. Shame when anybody gets killed."

"He got his car shot up about the same time yours was. You remember when I was here last?"

I spoke up. "You said it was high school boys did it."

Pawpaw looked at me, then his eyes lit up. "That's right, those high school boys. They gone too far this time, huh sheriff?"

"I'm not sure it was them."

"You not sure?"

The sheriff kicked a clod of dirt into the water. "His neighbor saw the shooting. But he was some distance away, plowing under his corn crop. You know the feds pay you not to grow corn."

"Sounds like easy work," Pawpaw said.

"Yeah it does. Anyway, this neighbor says it was a woman. She didn't mess around either. Just flat out plugs him, no reason whatsoever."

"Well now, he was naked, you said."

"Un huh." The sheriff looked toward the house. "You think that might be the reason?"

Pawpaw shrugged. "Could be."

"Is Lidia here?"

"Oh yeah. She's probably passing the Hoover around."

"Think I might like to talk to her. That is, if you don't mind."

"She don't know nothing about it."

The sheriff smiled, and it looked like some of his leather might flake off when he did. "Yeah, she probably don't, but maybe she heard something. You know how women talk."

"Yep. They sure do."

"And this could be tied to a string of shootings."

"That right?"

"Eight men in the last ten years. Nine with Maurice."

"They all dead?"

"Yep. And all with the same gun."

"That sure is something. A woman."

"Yep. That's why we never got anywhere. So it's lucky we finally got a witness."

"He saw her good, huh?"

"Not too good, but he could see she wasn't a man."

"So you don't know who she is?"

"Not yet."

Pawpaw thought about this, packing down some dirt with his boot. "You might be fishing with an empty hook, sheriff," he said finally.

"Yeah, could be. But I've always been a pretty good fisherman."

25

THE AFTERNOON was blistering, and since we were now hidden by Pawpaw's levee, Jute and me stripped off our clothes and jumped into the cold water. Well, Jute stripped off his, all of them, but I kept on my underwear. I was too old to be naked, Memaw said. Except in the bathroom, of course, but nobody could see me in there, if I'd just remember to close the door.

Jute couldn't swim that well. His swimming was mostly pointing his head in one direction and flailing his arms so that he headed off in yet another direction. His bowlegs were useless to him in the water; they just trailed behind him like frog legs. But as Pawpaw said, you couldn't drown that boy because he floated like a cork. You could even tie a line to him, bait it, and catch fish.

Not in Charlie's Hole, though—no fish in there that I could see.

We played all the regular water games—blind the boy, pull him under and drown him, and various games of skill, such as spitting. Then we sat on the crusty rim and enjoyed the sun. I told Jute stories about what school was like, and this was endlessly fascinating to him. Eating with a hundred other kids in a big room with cold air blowing from holes in the walls so that you shivered. Fighting blood-thirsty desperadoes in the schoolyard. Coloring on paper without lines. But he was most interested in the board of lower education. How bad did it hurt, he wanted to know. Did Mr. Faat whip you every day? How many times? Did he whip the girls? Did he whip the teachers, even if they were bigger than him? No detail was too trivial. I told him about the red paint that had worn off and now looked like a splatter of blood.

"Maybe it is blood," he whispered.

"Maybe it is," I agreed. And he had a point. I'd never seen the board when it was new and freshly painted, which was even before I was born.

I was getting hot just sitting there, so I stood up. "Race you," I said, and dove in.

"Hey!" Jute cried. "Cheater! Cheater!"

I made it across in no time and looked back. Jute was thrashing as usual, not making much progress, so instead of swimming back, I dove down to see how far I could go. Maybe I could find the center of the earth. I closed my eyes because the water was getting saltier all the time. Just as my ears pop-popped, my head collided with something. Suddenly I was staring into the eye of a sea quench. A black eye, gigantic and unblinking. I yelled, but yelling made no sound, only bubbles. I clawed desperately at the water as I rose, and now the quench was grabbing at my feet.

Trying to pull me down! I broke the surface and Jute was right there, still struggling across.

"The quench!" I yelled. "The quench!"

"The what?"

"The monster!"

I shouldn't have said that because Jute started crying and screaming. And by the time he made it to shore, both Pawpaw and Memaw were running toward us.

26

LATER, BACK IN THE HOUSE, Jute said I should get whipped for scaring him, but I said I really saw it.

"Just an eye?" Pawpaw said.

"Uh-huh. I didn't want to stick around."

He sat back in his kitchen chair and lit one of his cigars. The smell of sweet hay and cherries wafted over, and I breathed deep.

"I believe you, Charlie," he said finally. "And your teacher told you about this thing?"

"She told me about the sea quench. It has twenty-six arms and big black eyes."

"She wouldn't tell you a lie, I guess."

"No sir she wouldn't."

"Well, if it is a sea quench, that means this hole is connected with the ocean by an underground tunnel. And if sea quenches can come up from the ocean, so can sharks."

"Like man-eating sharks?"

"Like naked boy-eating sharks."

I shivered. Memaw put a glass of apple cider in front of me. "Drink this. It'll cut that water you swallowed."

I drank it and it tasted salty at first, then I kept drinking and finished it. I noticed Jute in the living room, wearing a long t-shirt and fresh underwear. He was still sniveling with his nose almost touching the screen. His face flickered with colors.

Memaw stood up straight and cocked an ear. "Car's coming."

I heard it too—a car rattling over the cattle guard of our driveway. I ran to the door and looked out. "It's the sheriff." Nobody said anything. When I turned around, Memaw had collapsed in the chair next to Pawpaw, her face looking gray. Pawpaw was wiping his own face with a handkerchief. A hot breeze was blowing through the screens.

They sat there waiting for the sheriff, but then I heard Lona's voice from the car. "It's Lona and Uncle Dan!" I cried. "With the pigs!"

"Can this day get any worse?" Memaw said.

27

MEMAW PROBABLY THOUGHT Uncle Dan had been arrested by the sheriff and he was bringing Dan home like he brought my daddy home so many times. But the sheriff wasn't there and it wasn't his sheriff's car neither.

Neither sheriff nor pigs in that car.

"Pigs?" Dan said. "I never said anything about pigs." When he went back to the driver's side, I noticed the front grille was crunched in. It was steaming and speckled with feathers; duct tape was holding the hood down. Uncle Dan slammed the door and came back to me. "Here's a bag of ham biscuits," he said. "Lona didn't want 'em."

Taking it, I turned to hide my disappointment.

"Charlie," he said, and I assumed he was gonna tell me I didn't thank him. But how could I thank a liar? "Charlie, I want you to meet your new aunt."

"I already did that."

"This is another new aunt."

"Oh…" I turned around and stared at her.

"Hi Charles," said a tall woman with straight black bangs.

"You can call her Mary," Lona said sourly. "No need for formalities."

Mary, like my mother Mary! True, she didn't have my mother's hair. Her nose was bigger and her eyes were too close together. She was taller and not as dark. But none of that mattered, 'cause when she spoke it was my mother's voice. My mother's voice! The dead didn't have to stay dead, I thought. Pawpaw didn't know a thing. Jesus rose from the dead, didn't he? And somebody else I'd learned about in catechism—Larry somebody, who rose from the dead too. I stared at this too-tall Mary even as Pawpaw and Memaw came up and hugged Lona and shook Mary's hand. They were acting like they didn't know her either. Even so, I kept waiting for Uncle Dan to say, *Don't you recognize her, Charlie? Don't you recognize your own mother?*

But he never said that. They'd all gone inside and I was still standing there, clutching that bag of biscuits.

28

WHEN I FINALLY WENT IN, they were sitting in the living room, talking. Jute still had his face plastered to the screen, but now the sound was off. Dan was smoking a cigar and Pawpaw was smoking a cigar, and all the women but Memaw were smoking too. I moved behind the sofa and inhaled every time a cloud came my way, while watching Mary who was my mother Mary. She wore a white blouse and blue lady pants, and a string of pearls like ladies do, but now I noticed that her eyes were blue like her pants, while my mother's eyes were brown like pecans. This confused me, I'll admit. But then I thought, if Mary had been to heaven to see Jesus, wouldn't Jesus have given her blue eyes like she had now, and that perfect white skin?

"Mary works in the statehouse," Uncle Dan said. "Isn't that right, Mary?"

"It's nothing really. I escort tour groups around. Show them the holes Dr. Weiss made when he shot Huey Long."

"The son of a bitch deserved to be shot," Memaw said.

"Now Lidia."

She glared at Pawpaw and he turned away from her and relit his cigar, even though it was still burning. "He hated us, he and his brother," Memaw said. "They hated everything French. Look at Charlie and Jute. They'll never be *Français.*"

I wasn't sure why those words hurt, but they did. I didn't know why the French thought they were better than the Anglos, or why the Anglos thought they were better than the French. But somebody was always saying he was better than somebody else and getting into a fight about it. That was always the way it was.

"I just show people the holes," Mary said. "It's not a cultural statement or anything."

"Uh-huh." Memaw got up and went into the kitchen.

Pawpaw leaned forward, took his cigar out and tapped ashes on the floor—what he often did when Memaw wasn't looking. "She's under a strain. The day hasn't gone that well."

"I hope we haven't added to it," Mary said.

"Oh no, not at all. Not at all." He sat back then, but didn't smile.

"That's a nice painting," Mary said. We all looked where she was looking, at the painting of the Louisiana mountain that didn't exist. And I wondered how she could forget her own painting like that. *And* her children.

"Funny thing," Dan said. "My brother had a wife named Mary, and she painted that the year she disappeared. The same week, actually."

"I'm sorry to hear that."

"It was my brother's fault that she—"

"She painted it in the field out back," Pawpaw cut in.

"It looks so real," Mary said, "I'd assumed it was painted from life."

"Oh no, ain't no mountains out there. A lake, but no mountains."

"What lake?" Uncle Dan said.

"Charlie's Hole, that one. Course, it wasn't here when you left."

"When I left? You mean three years ago?"

"No, three days ago."

"What on earth are you talking about?"

"Maybe you want to tell them, Charlie?"

"I do?"

"Sure. Tell them how you dug that hole with no bottom."

So I told them how Jute and me dug a hole with spoons and it filled up with water, and then Pawpaw tried to measure how deep it was, but he couldn't because the earth is a coconut.

"Charlie's right. I tried to measure it with a rope and ran out of rope at sixteen fathoms." Pawpaw glanced over at Lona. "A fathom is five feet."

"It's six feet you said before," I said.

"That's right. Charlie's right."

"Jesus," Uncle Dan said. "One hundred feet you're saying."

"Ninety-six feet," I said.

"Is this just a story, Charlie?" said Lona, who might've gotten the idea, like Mrs. Bertrand did, that the Boones weren't to be trusted.

"Oh no," Pawpaw said. "It's right there in the field. You want to see it?"

Uncle Dan stood up. "Yeah, sure. Let's have a look at Charlie's Hole." He glanced over at me and winked, and at that moment I forgave him for forgetting the pigs. I couldn't stay mad at him for long.

29

Except for Jute, who was glued to the television, we were all standing on Pawpaw's three-foot levee, looking at the water. Uncle Dan stepped down inside on a dry part, dipped a finger and tasted it.

"Does tastes like seawater," he said.

"It keeps getting saltier all the time," Pawpaw said.

"That's kinda strange."

"Nature's strange, that's for sure."

"There's a sea quench in there," I said. "I saw it."

Uncle Dan looked over at me. "A sea quench?"

"Uh-huh."

"And what does a sea quench look like, Charlie?"

"It's pink and has a hundred arms. And a big black eye."

"Just one eye?"

I tried to remember what Mrs. Bertrand had said, but that

got all tangled up with my own thoughts about it. "I think it has three. But I just saw the one. The left one."

One side of Uncle Dan's lips curled up like it always did when he thought something was funny, and I knew that he didn't believe me.

"A hundred feet deep," he said to himself.

"It might be a lot deeper than that," Pawpaw said. "That's all I had rope for."

Mary seemed fascinated in it, or in something, anyway. She walked along the levee, looking down and every which way like people do when they're considering buying a property. Memaw tossed something in the water—her gun, I think it was—then she and Lona started back to the house, talking. Most women didn't like to butt in on man talk anyway, especially if it was about how high or deep something was, or other facts of nature. Or sports. Or a lot of other things I could mention.

"The sheriff said I should get this professor from Lafayette to look at it," Pawpaw said.

"Is that right?"

"Some fellow writing a book."

"When did he say that?"

"This morning."

"Whatever brought him out here, I wonder."

"Probably that naked man who got himself shot. The sheriff wanted to talk to Lidia about it, but she was lying in the bed. She was under the weather most of the day."

"Flu?"

"I dunno. Something."

"So he'll be back?"

"The sheriff? Most likely."

Uncle Dan massaged his chin with two fingers and looked over toward the house. Then he looked at the barn.

"Think I'm gonna put that cruiser in Charlie's Hole. You mind?"

Pawpaw shrugged. "Why not. It's bottomless."

30

Uncle Dan couldn't get the police cruiser up Pawpaw's levee. The dirt was too fresh, he said, and the hump was too high. Pawpaw said he'd get his tractor and push it in. Lona came running from the house with her skirt flapping around her and said what the hell was he doing because her purse was in there. She opened the front door and got it out, and her clothes. Even as she walked off, Pawpaw asked if anybody wanted anything in the car, they might want to get it now before it was too late.

"They usually keep guns in the trunk," Mary said. "Tear gas and shotguns."

"I don't want any of that," Uncle Dan said. "It's all stuff they can trace."

"You wanna see what's in there," Pawpaw said, "I could hammer out the lock."

"No, just push it in."

"A car's coming," I said. I was real good at picking them out from a distance, from the yellow plume of dust beyond the trees. This seemed to worry Uncle Dan.

"Push it in," he said. "Come on, Dad, push it in!"

Even the tractor couldn't get the cop car to go up the levee, so Pawpaw backed up and slammed into it. On the second try the car went up and slid halfway on its undercarriage, where it tilted like a seesaw. With the bashing, the trunk sprung open, and I guess that trunk door made the difference. Like the sail on a sailboat, it caught the wind, sending the car sliding over the other side and into the water. The car stopped, inched forward, then eased in and floated. Air hissed from the seams. If there were guns in the trunk, I couldn't tell on account of that laundry bag.

Uncle Dan was more interested in the car coming up to the house, and now he could probably see what I saw—that it was Father Martel and not the sheriff. Suddenly he looked back at the cop car and yelled, "Great day!"

He leapt into the water with all his clothes, even his boots, but whatever he was trying to do, he was too late—the car had gone down. He dived into the bubbles and foam, and was gone a good long time. Mary stood behind us, wanting to know why he'd jumped in like that, but we didn't know. Pawpaw said he hoped he didn't get his fingers stuck in something and get dragged down. I was about to say the quenches might get him when Uncle Dan popped back up, gasping and spitting water. The funny way he was swimming—hitting the water with the flats of his hands and hardly moving his legs—he reminded me of Jute.

Uncle Dan couldn't get out any better than I could, so Pawpaw and me helped him. He sat on the levee with his head down, his hands on top of his head, slapping his head like he was killing mosquitoes. He looked depressed, or maybe he'd got water in his nose and almost drowned. If I'd almost drowned, I'd be depressed too.

"It was in there all along," he said. "I had it and throwed it away." He suddenly looked up at us. "Don't tell Lona about this."

"Okay," I said, but I didn't understand why. Since he was all sloppy wet, wouldn't she see he'd fallen in?

As he squished to the house in his water-logged boots, he said to Pawpaw, "I saw a horse in there, 'bout thirty feet down."

"A horse," Pawpaw said.

"Was it Lunch Time?" I said. I almost didn't get that out with the lump in my throat.

Uncle Dan looked back at me and said it probably wasn't. "Lot of stray horses around here, Charlie."

I wanted to believe him but I couldn't. I'd never seen stray horses except during Mardi Gras, when riders fell off them from too much beer. Uncle Dan said that's where Pawpaw got Lunch Time to begin with—a drunk jumped off to chase chickens, caught the biggest one and rode it home. That was when the world was young, when chickens were bigger than they are now. So big he even forgot his horse.

I didn't believe that because nobody would forget Lunch Time, didn't matter how big the chicken was.

31

Now it was the barn for Jute and me. Pawpaw got out the cots from the Army Surplus store and set them up in the loft.

"I don't even have a bed now," I said.

"It's a cot like soldiers use. Just pretend you're a soldier."

"I don't want to be a soldier."

He sat on my cot next to me and put his hand on my knee. "The governor didn't have a bed until he was nine."

"I'm nine, and I always had a bed till now."

"So there you go. You're way ahead of the governor."

"Except I'm going backwards."

"Everybody takes his own path, Charlie. And maybe you'll be governor one day too."

"If snakes don't get me."

"There's no snakes up here, so dry those tears."

He was right about the snakes. The loft was too high for bugs too, and a breeze blew through the open doors on each side most of the time, so it was cooler than the house. Or at least it wasn't as hot. If I lifted my head, I could even see the pasture and the hole I'd dug. Right now I could see the moon shining off it, like there were two moons.

Jute twisted around in his cot and asked why Father Martel didn't have children if he was a father. I told him that Catholic fathers didn't get married, so they didn't have children. Then he wanted to know if our own father was Catholic, and I said yes, though something about that didn't make sense, even to me.

Father Martel had never come to our house before to take confession. Usually you had to meet him at the church and talk to him through a brass screen in a box. But this time he'd come and talked to Memaw in her bedroom with the door closed, and afterward I saw her with her rosary beads. She was fast with them because she said the prayers in French, and French doesn't have as many words as English. She needed only two minutes to go all the way around with the fifty-nine beads waving and clicking, but she still needed all evening to do her penance. Like a thousand prayers. Maybe more.

Jute had gone silent now, so I got up from the cot and went to the loft door and sat there on a hay bale, watching the house. I had two malted milk balls left from a box Lona had given me, and I nibbled them, making them last. On the porch, somebody was rocking in that broken-down rocking chair, smoking, the red dot going up and down, up and down. In my old room the light was on, and I saw Uncle Dan standing there with his face to the glass. He turned and said something I couldn't hear with all the crickets and cicadas, then the light went out. On the porch the red dot sill went up and down and I figured it was Mary out there rocking. Even though Uncle Dan had flipped over the mattress and Memaw put on new sheets, it probably still smelled like pee. You could hardly expect a lady like Mary to sleep on boy pee—not unless she was the mother of the boy who peed. But if she wasn't the mother, then she was just a liar who pretended to be the mother.

I thought about this and many other things, and eventually I may have fallen asleep sitting there, because I saw Lunch Time pull herself out of that pool, shake herself off and run about in the pasture. Gamboling through straw weeds like a newborn pony. She was glowing white in the moonlight even though she used to be brown. Then she went back to hole to drink, and that's when the quench lunged from the pool with all its arms waving and grabbed her, pulling her in. Then the quench saw me in the loft and came out, making a chalk-line for the barn, smacking all those wet arms on the ground—thup, thup, thup. At the barn door it began jumping, trying to get up to me. I tried to move but couldn't.

I woke to find Jute shaking me.

"I can't sleep," he said.

"Because you're afraid of snakes?"

He shook his head. "'Cause you keep moaning."

I went back to my cot and lay there till the cock crowed on the next farm over, then I fell asleep.

32

FOR BREAKFAST, Mary made us beignets from scratch. She said she once worked for a restaurant that served only coffee and beignets, right after she graduated from Newcomb. That was a good school for potters and poets, she said, but not much else. I asked what she did now, and she said she was a tour guide, and if I'd been listening I'd already know that. I guess I'd asked because I thought she was lying. Which she was, one way or the other.

She said go ahead and eat my breakfast, as there wasn't a more nutritious breakfast than flour and sugar. A doctor by the name of Kellogg proved it years ago. Before then everybody was just skin and sinew.

"I like sugar," Jute said. He had the bowl of sugar Mary had ground up and was spooning that powdered sugar into his beignet. If you want to know, a beignet is just a donut with the hole inside so you can't see it. But once you tear it open you can fill up the hole with fig jelly if you want. Or strawberry jam. But if you want sugar, that goes on the outside, as everyone knows.

"You're supposed to put the sugar *on* the donut," I said.

"It's better on the inside."

The older Jute got, the more ornery he became. I liked it when he did everything I said without argument.

"I wish we lived on a sugar farm," he said, "and ate all the sugar."

"You don't grow sugar on a farm, you dope, you dig it out the ground."

"Oh."

"Actually," Mary said, "you do grow it. You know all that sugarcane around New Iberia?"

I didn't, but that didn't keep me from arguing. "Sugarcane sucks sugar from the ground, so it comes from the ground."

"No, Charles, the cane is a plant that makes its own sugar. Then the farmers crush the cane and dissolve out the sugar."

I looked at Jute, whose face was now totally white below his nose. He was grinning, his red gums looking strange in that white face, like he was from a circus.

"Your uncle is thinking of planting that field out there in sugarcane. That isn't a bad idea, as the price of sugar is going up."

"How come?"

"Because of those missiles in Cuba. If the president blockades Cuba, we won't get any more sugar."

"What if they shoot off those missiles?"

"Then you won't have to worry about the price of anything."

"I won't?"

"Nobody will. If that happens, we'll all be dead."

Jute didn't say anything, but he leaned over the bowl of sugar and I could tell he was trying to keep from crying.

33

Lona drove me to school and Mary came along as she had to pick up some things if she was going to be staying with us.

"Are you really my aunt?" I asked her.

"No, Charles. That's just something your uncle said."

"Then who are you?"

"I'm Mary, like I said."

"Don't ask all those questions," Lona said. "It's rude."

I lay over in the seat so I wouldn't have to see either one of them. I decided I didn't like Mary, and not just because I was sleeping in the barn, which I'd discovered was actually better than sleeping in pee after all. I didn't like her because I'd thought she was my mother and now I thought she wasn't.

"You ought to sit up, Charles," she said, glancing at me. "Young men sit up."

I sat up but I didn't like it. And I didn't like her calling me Charles all the time. I hated that name.

Mrs. Bertrand said that instead of math we'd have a drill on safety procedures for when the bomb landed on us. The whole state was doing this after the governor said Louisiana was the first place the Cubans would attack with their Russian missiles. They wanted to burn up our sugar plantations and oil fields, which the country depended on.

Mrs. Bertrand set up the projector and showed us a film of Mr. Wizard saying that radiation was natural to the environment and we shouldn't be afraid of it. Color televisions put out radiation. Even wood and bricks of houses, the air we breathed and the food we ate, they all had radiation. Even if you didn't eat or drink and lived outside and didn't watch television, you were still bombarded by invisible cosmic rays from outer space.

You couldn't escape it, and it was good.

Then we watched a cartoon from the government that showed how the three little pigs survived a nuclear blast by hiding under sturdy oak desks and covering their eyes with their hooves. The film wasn't over when Mr. Faat came on the intercom and said we were under attack and we were all to go to a civil defense shelter.

Mrs. Bertrand looked up at the speaker box. "What did he just say?"

"He said we're under attack," I told her, "and to go to the defense shelter."

"No. This is a drill. This is just a drill." She cut off the film but she didn't do it right. The film broke and began flapping. Still in the dark, she hit the projector and its cart gave out, sending the projector crashing to the floor.

Mr. Faat came back on the intercom and said that this wasn't a drill. "I repeat," he said, his voice all quivery, "this is *not* a drill."

A boy turned on the lights and opened the door to the outside hall. I now heard the air-raid siren starting up downtown at the courthouse, which was six blocks away.

"Jesus," Mrs. Bertrand said. "Oh fucking Jesus."

"You said a bad word," Lucy Quibodeaux said.

Mrs. Bertrand ignored her. "Mousey," she said to nobody in particular, pushing children aside to get down the aisle. "I have to find Mousey."

"I think we're supposed to get under the desks," a boy said. "Like the pigs—"

"Oh shut up," she snapped. She went out into the hallway. I could see other teachers out there now. Students were dribbling into the hall even though they were supposed to stay in their rooms. Some were crying. Mousey came up and Mrs. Bertrand grabbed him and hugged them. Then she dragged him off.

A couple of boys and me went to the door and watched them head for the main hall that led outside. "We better follow them," somebody said.

"Uh-uh," said a girl behind me. "We're supposed to get under the desks and cover our eyes."

"Then where are they going?" I said, before running after Mrs. Bertrand. When I looked back, I saw the better part of the class pouring out with their book bags and their Tony the Tiger lunch tins. But a few were probably doing what the three little pigs did, what the government told them to do. I knew one thing, though—this old school wouldn't stand up to an H-bomb attack for very long.

34

THE MAYOR'S CONSTRUCTION COMPANY had built the fallout shelter on the courthouse grounds where the Pinkerton men almost shot down that famous editor who robbed banks and trains—I forget his name, but he just barely got away. The two grass-mowing machines that were stored in there were now in the weeds where the mayor had pushed them. I'd seen him doing it from across the street and two blocks down. As he closed the door behind him, Mrs. Bertrand yelled for him to wait, then she and Mousey started running, along with the rest of us—half my class dropping their books and lunch tins to run faster and crying for their mothers. Mrs. Bertrand broke her heel in the road and fell. Then a girl fell on top of her. Mousey and me got there first and started banging on the door.

"Let me in," Mousey yelled. "I'm in the fifth grade."

Thinking Mousey might actually know something about getting into fallout shelters, I shouted, "And I'm in the third grade!"

I heard a garbled voice in there, but I couldn't tell what it was saying. We began banging on the door again, now joined by half a dozen third graders. And then Mrs. Bertrand hobbled up and told us to quit all that banging. We stopped and formed a sniveling ring around her as she shouted through the door.

"You have to let us in. These are children. You want them to get burned up?"

"I'm not buying that, you goddam Ruskie."

"What are you saying? I'm Ida Bertrand. This is my class at RC Elementary."

If he said something I couldn't hear.

"Let us in, come on."

"I can't."

"But we'll die out here!"

"This facility is only for city officials. It's illegal to let anyone else in."

"Bullshit!" Mrs. Bertrand shouted, and I was impressed with her language. "You're the only one in there."

"We don't have room. The whole council is in here."

"Yeah. Like who? Let me hear them."

Nothing.

"Let me hear Jerry Guillard. Or Otis Smith."

"Go away or I'll have you arrested."

The siren started winding down and Mrs. Bertrand looked around hopefully, but then it got to winding up again. A truck pulled up and two burly men jumped out. "They won't let you in?" one asked.

"The mayor's in there," Mrs. Bertrand said. "He's in there by himself."

The other scratched the black stubble on his cheek. "We can bust it open if you want."

"I don't know if you can. It's bomb proof."

The first man winked, herded the children aside, then both of them ran at it together, lowering their shoulders. The steel door snapped off its hinges and slammed down, knocking the mayor back against storage cabinets. He fell and didn't get up. Mrs. Bertrand and the class piled in, but there wasn't enough room, even with some of them standing on the door and others standing on the mayor. Outside were those two men, along with two girls—the Fontenot twins, who were bawling because they knew they were going to die—and me. I was wondering what good a fallout shelter was without a door when one of the men said it wasn't much good at all.

"This ain't much good without a door."

"Should we put it back up?"

"Shit no, man. We gotta get outta here."

And they did. Their truck took off down the road, headed out of town. I took off too, running up the courthouse steps. That brick building would be better than a fallout shelter anyway, especially one with no door and a mayor who was gonna arrest everybody crammed in there just as soon as he woke up.

35

Lona

LONA AND MARY had been shopping in downtown
Red Church while Charlie was watching Mr. Wizard explain
how radioactivity could cure cancer. They hadn't bought anything, but Lona had managed to get most of what Mary needed
anyway. Mary was queasy about shoplifting all that stuff, and
Lona found that funny, coming from a murderer.

"I'm not a murderer," Mary said evenly.

"Then what were you doing in that police car with your hands
tied behind your back? Why were they shooting at you? You
have to be wanted dead or alive for cops to shoot at you."

Mary didn't answer. Partly because she wasn't of a mind to
answer such questions—which she'd already made clear enough
on the way down here—and partly because of the civil defense
siren that was now wailing in her ears.

Lona slowed the car and watched as shoppers poured from

the double doors of Cohen's Fashion Emporium and looked around. One pointed to the sky and cried, "There it is! The missile!" When Lona bent forward to look through the windshield she smashed the Ford into a trash can and sent it rattling into the street. The car's engine died with an enormous backfire. This spooked the already edgy crowd, which went scurrying in every direction.

The government probably knew that running from an atomic bomb was just as useless as hiding under a desk, but they also knew people had to do something.

A man carrying a potted plant ran over from across the street, leaned in the Ford's missing door and shouted at them to take cover, bombs were falling on New Iberia.

The storekeep came out and tried to lock up but couldn't find the right key on his keychain. The accordion music playing on the store's loudspeaker cut out, and now the mayor broke in, breathless with excitement and patriotic fervor, saying America was under attack and he was manning the Red Church command center. Even now the enemy was trying to break down his door, Russians most likely, and the distinct sounds of banging on metal could be heard. "I'm not buying that, you goddam Ruskie—" With the clatter of a mike hitting concrete, his voice cut off. Now just the popping of static.

The storekeep dropped his keys and joined the general panic. Lona and Mary got out and looked up at the people running every which way, then at the silver glint of something far above.

"That's no missile," Mary said.

"It ain't?"

"It's a DC-8. You see those every day."

"Is it Russian?"

"Heck no. It's just a passenger jet."

Lona began to laugh and took Mary by the arm. "Come on then."

If Mary thought Lona meant to rob that fashion store, she was wrong, for they now headed across the street toward the wide open doors of the Gulf Coast Bank, where all the patrons had fled and the staff had locked themselves in the vault. Those bank employees would remain there for the better part of a week, since no one outside had the combination.

36

THE COURTHOUSE was two stories of bricks, and bricks had radioactivity in them according to Mr. Wizard. But it was American radioactivity, not the Russian kind. I imagined American radioactivity fighting Russian radioactivity, and wondered who would win.

On the open door was a flyer:

WAKE UP AMERICA!

MAYOR COOLIE THIBODAUX HAS INVITED THE PUBLIC TO A MEETING OF THE CITY COUNCIL FOR FRIDAY. THE CUBAN MISSLES WILL BE DISCUSSED. MEMBERS OF THE RC FIRE DEPARTMENT AND SHERIFF'S DEPARTMENT WILL LAY OUT THEIR PLANS FOR EMERGENCY PROCEDURES. HOT DOGS AND SODAS WILL BE PROVIDED.

I ran inside and up the creaking wood stairs. At the landing was a picture of Governor Jimmie Davis. He wasn't related to Jefferson Davis, the president of the Confederacy, but he was a good singer and wrote a song that trucks played from loudspeakers during the election. My mother loved that song, and I could still hear her singing it with me in her lap:

You are my sunshine, my only sunshine…

I glanced again at the governor's picture—he looked like most everyone else, like some rice farmer or some sugar farmer—then I looked down the hall.

Deserted.

"Anybody here?" I yelled.

No answer except for the siren blaring away on top of the building and horns honking outside. I pushed open the door to an office, then went through a doorway into the mayor's room. I knew it was his from the pointed straw hat hanging on the hat rack. People called him Coolie because of that hat. I also knew from the brass plate on the front of the desk that said, "The Honorable Mayor of Red Church."

I sat in his chair and opened his drawers. The first two had manila files and ink pens, but the bottom one had a box of Roi-Tan cigars and a half-full bottle of Wild Turkey, which was the whiskey that Pawpaw and my dad sometimes drank before my dad went up the river. When they drank it they would laugh and joke around most of the night.

I lit up one of the Roi-Tans and puffed on it. They were better than my uncle's cigars, and I thought if they toughened up my lungs enough they would protect me from the poison of the H-bombs.

"Charlie?" someone said. A girl's voice.

I stood and hid the stogie behind my back.

The Fontenot twins appeared at the door, their faces slick with tears. They both came running and hugged me from either side, which was funny considering I'd left them outside to get burned up by communist bombs. I held the cigar over my head to keep from burning them for real, then stuck it in my mouth.

Girls, I thought.

I knew all about Adam and Eve and how God made Eve from Adam's rib, but I couldn't understand why. There wasn't a girl in my class who wasn't smarter than me, at least on tests, but I bet none of them had ever caught a four-pound fantail carp, or gone riding bareback at midnight with a jar full of lightning bugs. They'd never been swimming in a leech-infested swamp or gone eye to eye with a sea quench without backing down.

Of course, I actually did back down, but that quench had the advantage on me, being underwater, and I wouldn't have run if he was on land. Except to get Pawpaw's rifle and shoot him.

I talked to the twins and they calmed down after a while. "Look," I said. "They're not gonna drop a bomb on our heads. They don't have enough bombs for that." I had no idea if this was true, but they believed me. And I told them, if a bomb did go off we'd see the mushroom, and we'd have plenty of time to look for a fallout shelter. Even this building might be good enough. According to Mr. Wizard, bricks stopped the three forms of radioactivity.

The girls knew that too, and Ann said, "Bricks stop alpha and beta, and some of the gamma. We just have to be careful not to breathe too much."

"What about the windows?" Amy said. "Should we close the windows and keep out the air?"

Ann looked at me and I said sure. Giving them something to do was the best idea of all. They stopped all that sniveling and flew around, closing windows, then closing and locking the doors. I don't know who had the idea of drinking the mayor's whiskey, but we did that, all of us. And then, when Amy found the deck of cards, I seem to remember that Ann had the idea of playing strip poker. Or maybe it was Amy.

Not that it made any difference.

I said strip poker was a bad idea, but they said we were all going to die anyway, so why not? I couldn't think of a reason that didn't sound like cowardice, so we played until we were all naked. I'd never seen a girl naked before, much less two of them, but being twins there wasn't much I could learn from Amy that I couldn't learn from Ann. One thing I learned was that girls didn't have pee-pees. I'd always thought they kept them tucked between their legs, but that was wrong. They had nothing down there. Nothing!

I got to wondering how they peed at all.

I must have fallen asleep, because I was dreaming of those naked Fontenot twins in the clutches of a sea quench when a nuclear bomb went off right overhead. Only it wasn't a bomb, it was the overhead light, shining in my eyes. I sat up and blinked. The room was spinning around me and I felt sick. The siren had stopped, which was good, but the sheriff and the mayor were standing at the door, which was bad.

Sleeping naked in the mayor's office with naked girls, that was also bad.

Dan

Dᴀɴ ᴀɴᴅ Gᴜs heard the siren when it first began, but neither one mentioned it. Besides, it was miles away, coming and going with the shifting breeze, and they were intent on what they were doing, throwing a two hundred foot rope into the water of Charlie's Hole. The rope was spliced together out of three pieces, and the end was equipped with a grappling hook Dan had welded together out of an old plow and parts from the other tractor that hadn't worked since Hurricane Audrey in '57. They fished around with the hook without finding the car—or the bottom—but did manage to snag something else. When Dan pulled it up with the six-banger John Deere—the rope threaded over a makeshift pulley—Gus called for him to stop. Dan cut the engine and came around to look. And there half submerged was Lunch Time, her big brown eyes now glazed over.

"Is Jute inside?" Dan asked.

"Yep. Watching cartoons."

"Well, let's get her buried quick. He shouldn't be seeing this."

They tethered her to the post, then Dan pulled off his boots and shirt, jumped in, and wrapped the rope around her girth. Keeping the tractor in low gear, they managed to get her out without the rope breaking, then Dan hooked up a short length of chain and they dragged her out the gate, past the barn and past the pecan grove. Out to where two other horses were buried, along with Dan's sister, Centipede, and his grandparents.

The horse dried out under the arid sun while Dan whittled out a hole for her with the tractor, and by the time he got done, Lunch Time had turned a ghostly white.

"What causes that?" Gus wondered.

"It's the salt," Dan said. "She got herself salt-pickled."

After they buried her, they headed back to the house, only to be met on the porch by Lidia, who was in an uproar about Jute.

"He's been in your room," she said. "Going through your stuff."

"Kids do that—"

"And he's swallowed bullets."

"He what?"

"He had this in his mouth"—she held out her hand, two saliva-sticky .38 caliber bullets in it—"and he had more in his pocket."

Dan took them from her, wiping them off on his sweaty shirt. "He'll be all right."

"Don't be so dang sure. When I asked him how many he had in his mouth, he said three."

"Shit."

"That boy will eat anything," Gus said.

"He can't eat bullets," Lidia said. "Bullets will kill him like—"
She clapped her hands since she couldn't snap her fingers anymore.

"What do you want me to do about it?" Dan said.

"Take him to the doctor."

"Suppose they want to cut him open?"

"Then you'll have to pay for it."

"Why me?"

"'Cause they're your bullets. You left them there for that boy to swallow."

"It's just one lousy bullet."

"How many bullets do you need to kill a person?"

Dan sighed and looked over at Jute, who was lying in front of the television. "This could be the most expensive bullet of all time."

Dan sat the boy on the sofa to question him, and soon discovered that Jute couldn't tell the difference between two and three. Unlike Charlie, who could count the blurs of fence posts when you drove by at fifty miles an hour, this boy couldn't count more than two fingers when you held them steady before his nose. Nevertheless, Lidia wasn't satisfied, so Dan rushed Jute to the doctor in Red Church. Or he would've rushed except he had to take the tractor, which wouldn't go more than twenty, and then he ran into a plug of cars coming the other way, loaded with folks screaming about Armageddon and missiles from outer space.

38

THE SHERIFF SAID I could have a lawyer if Pawpaw couldn't afford one. And I needed one because the infractions were serious. Very serious. We were in the sheriff's office and a sheriff woman was sitting next to me, darning a sock. The sheriff had pulled up an old swivel chair and began reading off a notepad.

"Criminal trespass—"

"I thought it was a fallout shelter."

"Don't interrupt."

"Okay."

"Let's see. Criminal trespass, second degree. Then we have a whole list of crimes after that. Truancy. Larceny. Underage consumption of intoxicating spirits. Underage consumption of tobacco products. Public drunkenness. Indecent exposure. Rape, two counts."

"Rape?"

"Other charges may be added at a later time." He turned the page.

"Rape?" I said again. While I knew it was about the worst thing in the world, even worse than murder, I wasn't sure what it was, exactly. Was it looking at a naked girl, was that it?

"Correct me if I'm wrong on any of this," the sheriff went on. "You were nine years old at the time of the infractions. You live with your grandparents, Gustave and Ezilda Boone of Red Church. Your father is Landry Boone—"

"But you know all that."

"—presently incarcerated in Angola, and your mother is Maria Arsenault Holster, of New Orleans."

"My mother?"

"We're going to have to lock you up, Charlie. Sorry, but we don't have any facilities particularly for children."

They fingerprinted me and one of the deputies grabbed the scruff of my collar like I was a stray cat and shoved me into a cage with flat iron bars going each way, with a ceiling so low I couldn't stand up. I'd seen a cage like it at the state fair, full of alligators from the Atchafalaya. And it reeked of pee, so at least those things were familiar.

I lay back on the hard cot and thought of Maria Arsenault Holster, of New Orleans. Of New Orleans, not of Red Church. And Holster was her name, not Boone like me. I guessed that meant she was married again. And if she was married again, that meant she was still alive, right? So Memaw's story of her taken by a hurricane was a lie. Wasn't nothing but a big fat lie. She'd run away and nobody wanted to tell me.

Why did she run, though? I wanted to think it was Jute,

because he was such a bad baby—colicky, they'd said—but I kept thinking of all the things I'd done, and I couldn't escape the thought it was me all along that made her want to go. And now, just as I'd found out she was still alive, I was dumped in jail like my father. I imagined him lying on a little cot like this one, in a cage where he couldn't stand up. Year after year. It was depressing, it really was.

39

Lona

THE GULF COAST BANK was giving away Mahatma-rice bags with toasters in them to new depositors, so Lona grabbed one, tossed the toaster, and yanked open a teller drawer. Empty, dammit. They were all empty except for the last one, which had a label saying, "Emergency Use." She laughed, for it was stuffed with fat stacks of bills still in their wrappers, and she wondered what they considered an emergency—some poor farmer wanting his money?

She counted fourteen stacks of tens and four of twenties—not as much as they'd filched from that bank in Baton Rouge, but it was a lot more than she had in her purse—less than two dollars and change.

The load wasn't that heavy, but she could feel the seams in the bag giving up. She tried to double bag it and called to Mary to help. But Mary wasn't going to help.

"I'm not getting involved," she said.

"You're kidding me, right?"

"I'm just an observer."

"Jeez," Lona said, finally getting the second bag over the first. Then she added a couple of toasters. "Can you at least get the door?"

Mary hesitated before pulling it open. "I'm opening the door as a matter of common courtesy. I'm not aiding and abetting criminal activity."

"Jeez Louise," Lona muttered, pushing by her.

An hour later they were stuck in traffic; the parish road that was normally deserted was now packed by the evacuation of an entire city. In front of them was a truck with a Victorian sofa in back. Pale, sickly-looking children were lined up on it. While they were stopped, a boy stood up, unzipped, and peed off the back.

Two horses galloped by.

"It's like Mardi Gras," Mary said.

"Really? I thought they had those big floats for Mardi Gras."

"Not in the country."

One of the horses turned around. Lona swallowed hard when the rider stopped at her window. "Ma'am," he said.

Lona looked up at him, almost blinded by the sun glinting off his badge.

"We're just going down the line here telling everybody we can get to…" The horse twisted around and he jerked the reins to bring it under control.

"You're telling people what?"

"That it was a false alarm."

"No missiles from Cuba?"

"That's right. Y'all can go home if you want." He clucked his tongue and rode back to the next car.

Cars and trucks were maneuvering to turn around. Only a few cars were still headed out of town, and the angry and frustrated folks of Red Church weren't of a mind to give them the right of way on that narrow parish road. It took another forty-five minutes to creep just two miles and turn off down the Boone driveway.

Inside the house, Lidia was listening to the mayor on the radio. "The Cubans aren't coming," she said, clicking it off. "It was all a mistake."

"That's what we heard."

"They're saying the principal of Charlie's school had a nervous collapse. He was most likely responsible."

"My gosh, is Charlie all right?"

"I don't know about Charlie, but Jute has a bullet in his stomach."

"Oh no!"

"Dan took him to the doctor."

"Good God. Who shot him?"

"He's not shot. He swallowed it."

"Oh…he's not shot."

"Is that dangerous?" Mary asked.

Lidia shrugged. "I never had a boy swallow a bullet, so I don't know."

"I don't either," Lona said.

"So he'll be all right?"

"If it doesn't go off."

"What could make it go off?" Lona said.

Lidia shrugged. "You can't shoot a bullet without a gun, that's what I always heard." She looked down at Lona's heavy bags. "You got your shopping done?"

"Yeah, I got *mine* done." Lona glanced meaningfully at Mary's back as Mary wandered into the kitchen.

Lona and Lidia talked a bit more before Lona carried the money bag upstairs and into her room. She locked the door, stripped off her clothes for a bath, and then, unable to resist, dumped the loot out on the bed. The toasters clunked together, and it was probably that small shock that set off one of the dye packs that were armed with flattened shotgun shells triggered by mousetrap springs—a device cobbled together by one of the bank clerks from an article in *Popular Mechanics*. The first explosion set off a chain of three more explosions, splattering Lona and the entire room with fine blue polka dots of indelible ink.

40

Dan

DAN FOUND THE DOCTOR'S FRONT DOOR ajar and no one there. He made Jute sit in the waiting room, then he opened the inside door to the clinic. Open doors lined the short hall, and Dan found the doctor beyond the second one, stretched out on a paper covered examining table, looking like a corpse. Dan held his hand above the doctor's nose.

The doctor's eyes flew open, and he coughed violently. "What the hell are you doing?"

"I thought you were dead," Dan said.

"Hell no, not yet, so don't rush me." The doctor sat up and swung his feet to the floor. He coughed some more and licked his lips, reaching in his shirt pocket for a pack of Kingstons. "All right" —he lit one up and waved the match, dropping it in the pack—"what seems to be the problem today?" He was much shorter than Dan, and peered up into Dan's nose as if he could see some disease in there.

"It's not me. It's my brother's boy."

"The flu?"

"Nah. He swallowed a bullet."

"He did, huh. You shouldn't let him do that."

"He gets into stuff."

"What caliber?"

"Thirty eight."

"Twenty two is better. Give him those."

"I didn't give him anything. He gets into stuff."

"Right, you said that. Well, have my nurse bring him in."

"She's not here. Nobody's here."

"What's that?"

"Nobody's here."

He looked at his watch. "What in tarnation's going on?"

"Don't you hear that siren? Everybody's on the road, evacuating."

"Oh yeah. Los Cubanos and their missiles." He laughed a smoker's laugh. "But you're here."

"Not a good time, I guess."

"Oh it's a good time, everybody running around with their heads cut off." With the cigarette in his mouth, he rubbed his face with both hands. "Okay, let's get to it. Let's see that bullet eater of yours."

JUTE'S SHIRT WAS OFF and he was standing behind an X-ray screen. The doctor flicked it on, and he and Dan looked at the vague outline of Jute's insides, lit up in green phosphor. "There's your bullet," the doctor said, tapping on the screen, "already in the small intestine."

"Is that a bad thing?"

"Not really, but it does limit the medical options. I can't pump his stomach now, so we'll have to let nature take its course." He pointed at splotches further down. "What are these things, I wonder."

"More bullets?"

"No…looks more like rocks." He glanced past the screen at Jute. "You haven't been eating rocks, have you boy?"

"Uh-uh," Jute said.

"Well, that's strange then, because somehow you got half a gravel road inside you."

"He'll eat most anything," Dan said.

"That true?" the doctor said to Jute. "You'll eat most anything?"

Jute shrugged.

"Well, I want you to stop. No more rocks. No more bullets. No hard candy, even. Okay?"

"No candy?"

"Not if you're gonna swallow it whole."

Jute nodded like he understood, but Dan wondered if he really did. The doc said a bullet was nothing to get excited about. It would pass if they took a few precautions. No roughhousing, for example. Wouldn't want that bullet clacking against those rocks, and better have him go outside when he needed to go. A bullet and the hard ceramic of a toilet wasn't a good combination. Oh, and feed him bread. A whole loaf if his mother could force it into him.

"Is toast okay?" Dan asked.

"Sure."

"Toast with syrup," Jute said.

"He's got a sweet tooth, does he?" the doctor said.

"He likes his sugar."

"Most boys do. But you ought to teach him to brush his teeth. Lucky these are baby teeth, because he's got a cavity in every one."

After the doctor, Dan took Jute with him to RC Elementary to pick up Charlie. Only, the school was deserted, so he drove around with Jute pointing out where Charlie might be, which wasn't too helpful. The streets were empty, and so were the culverts under them where Jute claimed to see Charlie hiding. A few parked cars, some with doors open. Furniture on sidewalks. Trash cans overturned. Papers blowing across the road like tumbleweeds. In the distance, a streamer of mill smoke licked the rooftops.

Finally, Dan drove the tractor past the sheriff's office. Plenty of cars there. People moving in the windows. He turned around and parked. He really didn't want to go in, but he figured they wouldn't be arresting people in the middle of a nuclear war. Not for trivial crimes like his, anyway. And he certainly didn't expect they'd arrest a nine-year-old boy.

41

THE ONE SMALL JAIL WINDOW was getting dark when I heard Uncle Dan's voice, and then the voice of a man I'd heard before—a lawyer they called Dee Tee after the disease he had. His real name was Mr. Abate. Mr. Abate defended Negroes at state expense, and lost most of his cases, according to Pawpaw. That caused grumbling among the blacks, not to mention editorials in the paper, but white people wrote letters saying if blacks wanted better lawyers let 'em pay like regular people did. Charity only went so far.

I wasn't black though, so maybe he and Uncle Dan was just talking. Now I heard his voice booming through the door.

"I don't goddam care what time it is. I wanna see my client."

I looked down the row of cages. I was the only one in there. I felt the Wild Turkey in my stomach scratching around, trying to get out.

"Got him in my office," the sheriff's voice said. "Oday Faat. You know him?"

"Of course I know him. That boy batted over four hundred."

The door creaked opened. Jute and Uncle Dan stepped in. Behind him, the sheriff and Mr. Abate were moving in the opposite direction.

"Uncle Dan, I didn't do what they said."

"They gonna whip you, Charlie," Jute said. "They gonna whip you till you bleed."

Uncle Dan grinned, pulled over a stool, and sat with his knees against the bars. "If you want me to punch him in the stomach," he whispered to me, loud enough for Jute to hear, "just let me know."

"You're not supposed to do that," Jute said. His eyelids grew fat with fear.

Dan glanced at him, gave him an oversized wink, them turned to me. "He's worried about his bullet."

"What bullet?"

"Never mind that. Why don't you tell me why you're in here."

"Okay."

And I told him what had happened, starting with the films Mrs. Bertrand showed us. He didn't care about Mr. Wizard, but he was keen on hearing how the mayor wouldn't let anybody in the fallout shelter, leaving third graders to be roasted by H-bombs. And how the mayor had whiskey in his office and left it unlocked where children could find it. He repeated what I'd said, saying it better than I'd said it, and I said that was right, because I did find it, and Uncle Dan said he was particularly interested in the mayor's deck of playing cards with the naked pictures.

"They didn't have naked pictures," I said. "They had the regular pictures. Kings and queens and one-eyed Jacks."

He leaned in close to the bars. "Listen to me, Charlie. They had naked pictures. Got that?"

"I guess," I said. "But I don't even know what they look like."

"I'll show you some tomorrow."

"I have to stay here?"

"Just tonight."

"I don't wanna."

"Remember this place when you think of doing something wrong."

"Do you remember it when you think of doing something wrong?"

He grinned. "Unfortunately, I didn't have the experience at an impressionable age."

Late that night they brought in Mr. Willis. Mr. Willis was a black man weaving so bad that two men struggled to get him lying down on a cot. They told him to "Lie there, Willis," and "Shut up, Willis," then they left. I could see him by turning my head, and I said, "Did they arrest you for rape?"

He laughed. "Oh no, they busted me for drinking after closing time. I told 'em I didn't know that bar was closed. The door was wide open."

"Memaw yells at me for leaving the door open."

He sat up and squinted at me. "Hell, you just a boy. What you doing in here?"

"They arrested me."

"For what?"

"For rape."

He studied me for a long time, then he said, "You look like a boy and you sound like a boy, but I guess you ain't one, huh boy?"

"Uncle Dan will get me out."

"Oh I don't know. You got to have a lawyer for that. You got a lawyer?"

"No."

"I always get Mr. Abate."

"Does he get you out?"

"Ho! Mr. Abate never gets me out, not once."

"Then why is he your lawyer?"

"'Cause he's free, that's why."

"Oh."

"Get yourself Mr. Abate, that's what I say."

"Okay."

"When he comes here I'll tell him."

"Thank you."

"No need to thank me. He gives me five dollars for that."

I lay back on the cot and closed my eyes. Mr. Willis started singing to himself—

I ax her for lemonade
She gimme gasoline

and after a while I said who was that he was singing and he yelled, "Howling Wolf!"

Singing seemed to exhaust him, though, and soon he was snoring. I wondered if I'd get like him eventually, so used to jail I could fall asleep not half an hour after they locked me up. It would be good to be that way, I decided.

42

I DIDN'T GET TO SEE those cards because instead of Uncle Dan, Memaw came by with Mr. Abate. Mr. Abate waved his hands and yelled some things I didn't understand, and after ten minutes of him yelling and them arguing back, they said enough of that shit and I was free to go. For now.

Driving me home, Mr. Abate said I couldn't go back to school because of the Fontenot girls' parents. They'd made a stink and gone to the judge to get an order.

"An order just for me?"

"That's right, Charlie. It's got your name on it and the great seal of Louisiana."

I couldn't help but feel some pride then, that the judge had taken note of me, and I wondered if that would make me famous.

"The word is *infamous*," Mr. Abate said. "That's the opposite of famous."

He said I couldn't even go within one hundred yards of the school, according to the order, and Memaw in the front seat made it sound like this was a terrible thing. But it wasn't. If I'd known the judge could keep me out of school, I'd'a done something a long time ago.

Mr. Abate looked at me in the rearview and said I shouldn't get all pleased with myself, because I'd also have to stand trial, and depending on how that turned out, I might have to go to reform school in Monroe. I said that didn't sound too bad, and he said it was bad all right. He said they paddled students there every day. Ten whacks before breakfast, just to get the blood flowing. I said did they have a board with holes in it, and he said he didn't know, but most likely, and I said it still didn't sound too bad.

It didn't sound bad at all, and I began to see all the advantages of being a juvenile delinquent.

DAN AND LONA had painted my room—their room, of course. I could smell the paint from downstairs. Before lunch I snuck up there and looked in. The walls were cornflower blue, which I didn't like much. Not so much for the color, but they had painted everything, even the floor and the ceiling. Even that old green chair.

With the new white sheets on the bed, going in there was like flying up in the sky.

I went over to the window and saw Jute outside in the field. He was squatting with his pants down, using the world as his bathroom, and I was afraid they'd find out how I got him started.

Especially since Uncle Dan and Pawpaw were standing by the gate, watching him. But nobody mentioned it to me. They even saw him do it again after lunch and didn't say a thing except Memaw said she thought he was doing better.

I was gone one day and the world turned upside down.

That first evening after I became delinquent, Uncle Dan set me down and told be how babies are made (which sounded so gross I wondered if this was another giant chicken story), and he asked if that's what happened with those girls. I said I didn't remember because of the whiskey, but I didn't think so. If something happened like that I'd sure remember. He said he expected that was right, but he said to promise him I wouldn't drink whiskey anymore or have anything to do with girls who drank whiskey, and I said I promised.

"Not until you're twelve."

"I promise, Uncle Dan."

Uncle Dan was very strict that way. Not like Memaw, who didn't care what I did as long as it wasn't in her kitchen, or Pawpaw, who didn't care about anything if it wasn't a fact of nature.

Later, Uncle Dan gave me a Bible. He said if I read it I would learn all I needed to know about where babies came from, and there were parts he hadn't told me about. The best parts, actually.

"In a Bible?" I asked, and he said this wasn't an ordinary Bible. It was an educational Bible. It was the primary form of sex education in America, if I wanted to know.

I actually didn't want to know. I put the Bible under my cot in the barn, intending never to open it. Now that my school days were over, I figured I'd never have to learn anything ever again.

43

"WE GONNA GROW SUGAR and I get to eat all of it," Jute told me the next morning as he crumbled toast into his bowl of molasses.

"Is that a fact?" I asked him.

He nodded and grinned with all his black teeth.

Jute got almost everything wrong, but not this time. We were building a fort out of hay bales in the barn since Lunch Time wasn't there to eat them any more, when a truck drove up our driveway. Dan and Pawpaw came out to talk to the driver, and Jute and me ran over there to see what he had in the back.

"It's sugarcane," Uncle Dan said. He grabbed a stick, broke it in half and tossed us the pieces.

The cane was thick and ugly, not like the red and white striped cane I'd imagined.

"Chew it," Dan said, "don't look at it."

This struck me as about as appetizing as chewing on the leg of a goat, and maybe it was a test to see how smart I was, but I did it because I always did what Uncle Dan said. I nibbled on one end, then looked up at him, grinning.

"It's candy," I said. I looked over at Jute who was apparently trying to dissolve his piece with saliva, because he was licking it like an animal. "Just chew it," I told him, but he turned his back on me and went on licking.

I THOUGHT MARY would be angry about what I'd done, since good boys didn't go around raping girls in the mayor's office, but she didn't say anything like that. She said I was a victim as much as those girls were victims, like the whole town had been victimized, and she would see to it the real perpetrators of this vile scenario were punished to the full extent of the law, which wasn't nearly severe enough, but never mind, she'd see to getting those laws strengthened.

I didn't know what she was saying, and I figured she'd taken to drinking whiskey like I had. Whiskey made you say things you thought were smart at the time, but later you couldn't remember why.

After she went upstairs, I heard the door close, and then the sound of a typewriter. I asked Jute where she got a typewriter, and he said the same man who brought me home gave it to her. Why would Mr. Abate give her a typewriter, I wondered, but that wasn't very high on my list of things to figure out, considering all the other mysteries that now occupied my brain.

44

Jute and me wore beat-up Coolie-for-Mayor hats while we helped Uncle Dan plant the field with sugarcane. Uncle Dan used the tractor to cut a ditch as deep as my hand the entire length of the field, then Jute and me laid seed cane end to end, and each time we finished filling a ditch, Uncle Dan came back with the tractor and covered it with dirt. I planted five thousand three hundred and thirty-nine canes in one day, and Jute planted no more than five. He ate a lot more than he planted and had to go to the bathroom three times.

"Go to the house," I said.

"Uh-uh," he replied, and wandered off to the fence, dropped his pants, then came back.

"How come you're doing that?" I asked as I grabbed a cane he was licking and slapped it in the ground.

"'Cause it's candy."

"No, how come you're going to the bathroom in the field?"

"I don't wanna die," he said.

"Who told you that?"

"Uncle Dan."

Jute was lying, because no way had Uncle Dan told him anything like that. On the other hand, Uncle Dan had driven the tractor right past him squatting by the fence, and didn't say a word.

A second mystery was how Uncle Dan could grow sugarcane by planting the cane sideways in a ditch. You didn't plant tomatoes that way, or any other plant I knew about. Uncle Dan just said that was the way it was done, and you let the sugarcane figure out which way to go. That didn't sound right to me. The sugarcane couldn't be that smart if it let itself get broke up and chewed by children without a fight. It didn't know up from down from sideways, no more than a Mars bar or any other kind of candy.

The biggest mystery of all was where all the water was going. The water level, which had threatened to spill over the levee for days, had now dropped by two fathoms, which was below sea level. Pawpaw said he'd called a man to come and look at it, and for us not to play around there because if we fell in we might never get out. We believed him too, so we stood on the levee and threw rocks from the driveway down in the water, because throwing rocks wasn't playing, as we'd been told before. Throwing rocks was serious.

45

A WEEK WENT BY without rain. Uncle Dan was getting antsy; without rain the sugarcane would never get started. It would just rot in the field. Nutria and moles would eat it, not to mention the thousands of bluebirds that Uncle Dan paid us to chase away. Memaw said don't chase bluebirds away, they were lucky, but Uncle Dan said the only luck he needed was rain. Memaw said if he needed rain she'd get the rain, and she called Father Martel and got him to say a prayer for rain at the Sunday mass. I thought the whole service would be for us, but it wasn't. It was just one sentence, asking Saint Swithin, the patron saint of rain, to supply rain for the Boones' sugarcane field. And then a prayer for the Boy Scout troop of Red Church, asking Saint Medard, the patron saint of good weather, that it not rain and ruin their jamboree. Memaw frowned and slapped her pewbook closed, making such a clap that ladies with feathered hats and painted faces turned and looked at her. I slid down in the pew and got to wondering who God favored more, us Boones or the forty seven boys in Boy Scout Troop Number Three?

With not a rapist or juvenile delinquent among them.

The answer came clear that evening when black clouds rolled in just before sunset. Lightning flashed and thunder rolled. Each time it did, the cicadas would stop and listen, then start up again until the next thunder. No rain, though, and I figured the boy scouts had us beat. But the next night we finally heard the first fat drops popping on the sheet metal roof of the barn. I pictured Saint Swithin wrestling with Saint Medard, Saint Swithin on top, and Medard looking a lot like Mousey Bertrand. More pops of rain. Cool air blew in and the clouds let loose. I'd never heard such a wonderful racket as all that rain on metal, and soon I fell sound asleep.

The sun was already up when I woke to Jute's shaking me.

"Charlie, Charlie, the sugarcane made the sugar!"

"It won't make sugar that fast," I said, turning over. "It's got to grow first."

"It did. It made the sugar."

"Leave me alone."

"Okay, but I get to eat it all."

"Fine. Eat it."

"None for you, Charlie."

I fell asleep again, but not for long, as I heard Jute wailing out there in the field, and the first thing I thought was he'd fallen in the hole.

46

Snow.

That's what I thought when I saw it, that I'd slept till winter and this was snow. Not that I'd ever seen snow before except once, and I was too young to remember it. Memaw had picture of me running around in diapers with my tongue out, catching snowflakes, and I remembered the picture, but not her taking the picture. But that's what the sugarcane field looked like, as if covered with the snow of that picture.

Now I saw Jute down there at the hole. The water was threatening to overflow again and he was lapping it up. He only stopped to sit back on his haunches and let off a howl so mournful you might've thought he was a wolf or a coyote, like we used to have before the town put a five-cent bounty on their tails and killed them all.

"What's wrong?" I yelled.

But he didn't answer, so I climbed down the ladder and ran over the crunching snow. Suddenly I stopped and looked down. My feet weren't cold; they were hot. I squatted and scooped up a handful of hot slush. I tasted it. Salty. It was salt, not snow. I ran over to the hole and saw the great streamers of salt that had poured out in the night. Like snow drifts, except they were salt drifts.

Jute was now lying on his side, slumped over with a disappointment so deep I'm sure it changed his life forever. His life from now on would be measured in two parts:

his sugar days

———————

and then his salt days.

Now I saw Uncle Dan and Lona on the porch. Uncle Dan came running, also barefoot, but Lona stayed put, I suppose to let us, the disposable sex, find out how dangerous it was. Uncle Dan stopped at the gate and did what I did, picked up a handful, smelled it, then tasted it. He tasted it again, then yelled to the house.

"It's salt!"

"What?"

"Salt! Goddamn salt!" He came over to the hole and walked around it to where Jute and me were.

"I thought it was snow," I said.

"The crop is ruined. You know that? All that work. Why did I think I could ever be a farmer?"

I didn't say anything because I'd thought that too. Anybody who planted sugarcane sideways didn't know what they're doing.

Uncle Dan walked past us as if in a daze. He kept saying the same words over and over, like he couldn't believe it.

"Salt," he said. "Goddamned salt."

DAYS OF SALT

47

THE HEARING WAS TO DECIDE just how bad I was and if it was safe for me to go back to school. I said I was real bad, and Mr. Abate said that was the wrong answer.

"If you say that, they'll think you *are* delinquent."

"But I am."

"No you're not. Okay?"

"And I don't want to go to school."

"I know how you feel, son. Sometimes school can be a bear, but believe me, it's better to go to school than not."

That wasn't very convincing, actually, because for me, the days before going to school were a paradise. Like Jute when he lived in his sugar paradise, and then it all turned to salt. Going to school was Jute's sugar and honey and molasses, all drying up into salt overnight and killing any hope of getting any sugar ever again.

"Anyway," Mr. Abate said, "they'll all be here. And you don't wanna disappoint your Aunt Lona, do you? Or your Uncle Dan?"

"No, I guess not."

"And your grandparents, you don't want them to cry when you get sent to Monroe, do you?"

I couldn't argue with that, but sometimes you wonder if you can do anything at all without making somebody cry. And if you worried about them and did something different, maybe somebody else would cry. Of course, nobody would actually cry about me. Mr. Abate was just saying that, hoping I wouldn't notice he was playing a trick on me. I turned and looked around the courtroom. Two girls in the back were waving—the Fontenot twins. Their daddy yanked their hands down. Then I saw Jute on the other side. And Memaw and Pawpaw, and Lona and Mary. They were all there, all right. Mr. Abate was going to question them to show what a good boy I was, and they were going to lie and lie.

At the other table was Mr. Lemmon, who was originally from Shreveport but got fired from his job there and had come here to put as many Red Church people in the state pen as he could, according to Mr. Abate. All to make a name for himself and get his reputation back. Lemmon glanced at me and gave me a look so hard and mean I would've run away except for the police guarding the doors. He meant to get me, I could tell that much. He wanted to get me and put me in the state pen, not in any reform school.

Mr. Abate leaned down and whispered not to be afraid of Lemmon, 'cause he'd make mincemeat of that bum. I would have taken heart at this, but I didn't because I didn't know what mincemeat was, and because Mr. Abate reeked of whiskey.

48

THE JUDGE MADE A SPEECH about how we were looking for the truth, and then Mr. Lemmon made a speech that was filled with lies from start to finish. He was supposed to be talking to the judge, but he spent most of his time talking to the packed courtroom, waving his arms and pointing at me like I was the most awful human child born since William T. Sherman, and if a person such as me were allowed to go on living in Red Church without being properly rehabilitated, no telling what might happen. Would anyone be safe, he wanted to know. Could the citizens trust their beloved and tender daughters to RC Elementary without having their clothes ripped off by such a monster child? Did they want their tender sons bullied and beaten up on the schoolyard by an ape boy with the strength of an adult?

Tough Lung Charlie, he sneered. Some called the boy that, and not surprising. A feral child raised without discipline or parents. With a mother who'd run off as far as anyone knew, and a father serving time in the Angola penitentiary. The boy was living in a barn like an animal, raised by an uncle who should, by rights, be in jail himself.

"Daniel Boone! A fine historical name, now sullied by this man whose wife—or concubine as many suppose—was once a naked model for pornographers. *Pornographers!*"

He nailed the word hard and the women gasped. Many of the men turned their heads to glance at Lona. Maybe wondering if they had seen her before in a magazine—a magazine they still had, probably, hidden in the garage.

"Yes," he went on, "it's proper to be astounded and horrified by such an un-Christian nest of villainy in our midst. In the good and honest town of Red Church. Even the Lord Himself has shown his displeasure with the Boones, for He has smitten their land with salt. As the Bible saith—"

"Objection, your honor. This isn't a church. He can't quote the Bible."

"Overruled."

"But—"

"Overruled, I said."

Lemmon smiled and continued his preaching: "As the Bible saith, 'Their land shall become a burning waste of salt—nothing planted, nothing sprouting, no vegetation growing on it. Like the destruction of Sodom and Gomorrah, which the Lord overthrew in fierce anger.'"

"Objection! Irrelevant, and he's not even quoting it right."

"Sounds both relevant and right to me," the judge said. "Go on, Mr. Lemmon. I find this fascinating."

And he went on. If he had been talking about anyone else, I

would've run out to get kindling for the bonfire. What an awful person I was! Mr. Abate put his hand on my shoulder and whispered that nobody was buying it, but when I looked around, people were leaning forward in their seats. They weren't struggling to stay awake like they did in church. And I wondered how Mr. Abate knew they weren't buying it. Looked to me they were eating it up like pure cane sugar.

After Lemmon got done, Mr. Abate stood up and walked back and forth for a while in front of the judge, until the judge told him either to say his piece or sit down.

"That boy!" he suddenly thundered, pointing at me, "might be the most notorious criminal ever to issue from the bowels of hell." He stopped and everyone looked at me. I slunk down in my chair. "Or he might not be so bad after all."

He said that "all these numerous incidents" had been blown out of proportion. I wasn't all that much worse than any other kid, or any of the adults here when they were kids. "Who here hasn't played doctor when they were children?"

The spectators looked at each other, either in confusion or revulsion, I couldn't tell.

Mr. Abate went on like that, minimizing my school disciplinary record as a mere misunderstanding, my leading the mob that had broken down the door of the civil defense command shelter, injuring the mayor, as no worse that Halloween hijinks. Who hadn't committed some childish infraction, all in fun?

When he used the word "committed," the judge turned and glared at me, and I wasn't sure if Mr. Abate was doing such a wonderful job. By the time the judge called a recess I was sure he was doing a terrible job, and I figured I would be seeing my daddy very soon.

49

I was partially right, because the judge said he had no need to hear any more; his stomach was not strong enough. And, as much as he felt I should be tried as an adult and sent to adult prison, according to state law I was a child and must be disciplined as a child. An unusually incorrigible and dangerous child if he'd ever seen one, but the law was the law, so he was ruling me delinquent and committing me to the Louisiana Training Institute for an indeterminate period, but not less than the time it would take them to rehabilitate me, which, from what he had seen, would probably be when I came to a violent end, or reached the age of twenty-one, whichever came first.

I didn't mind going there because my daddy had gone there when he was twelve and Uncle Dan had gone there when he was thirteen. The Boones were famous at that school, both for football and for bare knuckle fighting. And Uncle Dan said it was just like a regular school with lousy teachers where they whipped you every day. That didn't bother me, 'cause I couldn't imagine any principal with a stronger arm than Mr. Faat, or any teacher worse than Mrs. Bertrand, that old mule. I hoped there wouldn't be any bullies as bad as Mousey Bertrand, but if there were, I'd beat them up just like I did him. The whole idea of being incorrigible and dangerous was beginning to grow on me and make me feel powerful.

They'd washed and waxed a police car to take me to Monroe, and Uncle Dan slapped me on the back and shook my hand. He said I was a man now and to hold my head up. "Never let them get to you, Charlie." He handed me that Bible I hadn't opened yet and he said hold on to it because they wouldn't let me have much, in his experience, and that Bible might be my only friend.

Lona hugged me and said she was sorry I had to go. So did Memaw and Pawpaw, and Jute, who couldn't stop crying. He kept trying to tell me a joke, but he couldn't remember anything but the last line, and finally he said, "Get it? Get it?" Then he started crying again.

Mary just sat in the car writing away on a notepad. Which was fine with me. I didn't want her straightening my collar and telling me to be a perfect little gentleman. Wanting me to be fancy boy Charles so I could get walloped the first day.

Not that I didn't get walloped the first day, because I did. That was my initiation. A bunch of sixth grade boys got me in the cut—a place where the staff couldn't see—and beat me up. But beatings just made your muscles bigger, every boy knew that.

"Go on and beat me," I said. "You'll be sorry."

They didn't like anybody talking back so they pulled off my shoes and threw them on the roof. Which was fine with me too; I didn't like wearing shoes anyway.

Of course I got paddled for losing my shoes. Five whacks with a board half the weight of Mr. Faat's. A school with no girls, with pigs and chickens and a herd of beef, and a pansy weight paddle swung by a wiry headmaster who was close to retirement—this was going to be a breeze. And it was, especially after I discovered the naked pictures in Uncle Dan's Bible.

It started with a trickle of pimply-faced boys coming around, wanting to look at that Bible for a while, and pretty soon nobody would beat me up or pick on me because I was the Bible Boy. I even formed a Bible study group and the headmaster gave us our own room and our own Bibles to study from, but all the studying was from Uncle Dan's Tijuana Bible. The boys had to go to the bathroom a lot, taking that Bible with them, one by one. Looking at the girls in there. I didn't see what attraction girls were, even naked ones, but the other boys said give it time, I'd discover it for myself. I hoped not. I hoped I would never grow up and they'd let me live in this reform school forever. It was a paradise, it really was.

I shouldn't have said that aloud, though, because somebody laughed and said, "Dream on, Pig Slopper."

I was also called Charlie the Pig Slopper, if you want to know, because that was my job. I enjoyed it too. I gave every pig a name and every pig knew me and came running when I called them. George Washington Boone knew his name, and George Washington Boone the Second wouldn't come unless I added the last part. Pigs were as smart as the boys here, and smarter than most of the staff, so I hated when they took them away to kill them.

The boys gave everyone a name according to what they did. There was Maurice the String Boy, who kept string all over his body. He'd turn and look at me in janitorial class, and slowly pull twenty feet of yellow string from his nose. Then he'd use the end of it to clean his teeth.

Mosquito Boy would sit on the floor of the old gymnasium, trapping mosquitoes by pinching his skin. The mosquitoes couldn't stop sucking and would grow as fat as ticks before exploding.

And then there was Alligator Clay, who had somehow smuggled an alligator into school. He kept it in a water trough in the field, and only the bravest cows would use it with an alligator floating in it, even though it was only a baby.

Alligator Clay had a way of seeing into people. He had those same cold eyes that reptiles do, and he'd look straight though what other people saw and see the real you inside. He said I had, deep down, the heart of a pig, that I'd been a pig before I was born.

"I dug a hole for pigs once," I told him, "with a spoon, and it filled up with saltwater."

"What you dug," he said, "was a window."

"A window?"

"Beelzebub sweetens his pork with salt. You opened a window into his house."

"Could be a window," I said, "or maybe I punched a hole in his roof and he's hopping mad."

Clay thought about that for a while. "You wanna hold my alligator?" he said finally.

Alligator Clay and me became best friends and I learned more from him than I ever learned in class. Claiborne Toad was his real name, but real names didn't matter much among us boys. Only what you did made any difference.

50

According to the state of Louisiana, us boys were aimless and incorrigible misfits, thus suited only for work in banks as security guards and in state office buildings as maintenance men. Alligator Clay said his dream was to become a night janitor, because night janitors could take anything they wanted. "What do you want to take?" I asked him, and he said he would take rubber. If he were a night janitor, he could go through all the desks and take all the rubber bands. And once he had enough he'd make the biggest rubber band ball in the world, even bigger than the one they had in Kansas. But why, I asked, as I'd never met anyone before who had a goal in life, and this was mysterious to me. Clay said if you did something no one else had done, or made something bigger than anyone else had made, a man by the name of Guinness would find you and give you a certificate, and everyone in the world would know who you were and what you had done.

"I got a certificate," I said, and after dinner I showed him the paper with the great seal of Louisiana.

Clay took it and read it to himself, his eyebrows slowing rising. "This says you can't go to school. You can't even get close to it."

"That's right."

"Jeez."

He handed it back to me without saying anything more, but I could tell he was looking at me in a new way, as if I'd suddenly grown six inches.

Fact is, I did have a growth spurt at about that time, probably because of the piles of black beans and cornbread, and especially the cod liver oil they were giving us. Two tablespoons every morning, which left a rancid taste in my mouth that lingered all day. But with all that oil, the muscles in my arms grew harder even as my pants grew shorter. I had a constant itching to beat somebody up, and Clay said that was all part of becoming an adult. His daddy beat up his mother all the time, and him too, which was why he was in Monroe and not lazing around in a pirogue, catfishing on Teeneg's Bayou.

"You got sent here because your daddy beat you up?" I asked him while we were in the shower with a dozen other boys.

"I got sent here 'cause I stuck a knife in him while he was sleeping."

"I'll bet that woke him up."

"You'd win that bet all right."

"Did he die?"

"Naw, but he had to go to the hospital for a week. A social

173

worker came to see me and said best if I wasn't there when ole daddy came back. Said I could go live with a relative, 'cept none of them would have a boy that stuck people while they were sleeping, so the only other place they could send me was here."

"I got sent here for rape," I said.

He looked me up and down. "You look too little for that."

"I'm getting bigger every day."

"Uh-huh. I'll bet you don't even know what rape is."

"Do too."

"What is it then?"

So I told him what Uncle Dan had told me about sex, even though I couldn't remember doing any of it, and Alligator Clay was impressed. He said he had never done anything like that, but one day he hoped to. I said it was pretty good, but I figured once was enough. He said if I thought that then I'd never done it, because once boys did it that's all they thought about. He said he knew this for a fact, so if I wanted to think about anything useful, I better get it in now, because pretty soon all I'd be thinking about would be girls, and my brain would be destroyed.

I thought of all the adults I knew, and I began to suspect that Clay was right.

51

Dan

DAN BOONE WAS THINKING about Lona, worried what she was thinking about him, that maybe she'd made a mistake in busting him out of that Missouri jail. Of course there wasn't any actual busting involved. Dan had been on a litter pickup crew on a two-lane highway, and when Lona rolled slowly by, he'd just opened the back passenger door wearing his prison blues, tossed his spiked broomstick into the ditch, and off they went. Not much of a jailbreak, so when they heard the police downstairs in Lona's apartment building that evening, they were completely unprepared, that is to say, buck naked and making up for lost time.

"They could have waited five fucking minutes," Dan said, which rather missed the irony of his situation—that his escape was a five-year felony compared to the thirty days he was serving on a misdemeanor, of which he'd already served twenty five.

Lona told him not to worry; she had a hiding place. So, still naked, they squeezed through an opening in the ceiling of a closet. Lona was sitting on the plywood cover when one cop noticed it and rapped it with end of his billy stick. As it didn't move, he observed it must be nailed shut.

"Should we open it?" said another voice.

"Nah, not worth it. Nothing but pigeon shit up there."

Eventually, Dan and Lona heard the cops drive off, but still they waited for night to fall before coming out. The apartment was trashed, but several boxes of Bibles were still stacked up in a corner, and enough clothes to go outside without being arrested for indecency. The Roadmaster, which was parked in front, had apparently not been reported stolen yet, so they loaded it up and headed south toward Louisiana, a state that Lona imagined was some sort of paradise.

And it was, Dan thought, if you were into robbing banks.

Now in the Red Church History Museum, Dan reread the plaque in front of him. He'd paid 25 cents just to learn about this notorious criminal, this Eugene Bunch who robbed banks and trains, and he was starting to think that graduating to trains might not be a bad idea. Sure, they didn't carry boxes of cash like they used to—that business had been taken over by armored cars—but they still carried plenty of rich people, and rich people carried plenty of cash when they traveled. Better yet, no one robbed trains anymore, which meant there wouldn't be any security guards to worry about.

He studied the gun that had killed Bunch and taken off his brother's thumb, thinking if some fancy pants newspaper editor could rob trains without the proper background and training, how hard could it be for a guy like Dan Boone? Beyond that, bringing down a hundred ton locomotive would be like bringing down a rhino or an African elephant—a kill that would earn Lona's undying admiration, even while funding the family's new enterprise.

52

PAWPAW WROTE ME a letter every week, telling me what was going on with the farm, especially with Charlie's Hole. The man from the college had come by and said he'd never seen a fact of nature like that. He came back two days later with a geologist, who said a salt dome under the house had broke loose, and was rising up through the crust of the earth. In a hundred years it might reach the surface, destroying the house and the barn and everything standing there. That wasn't bad, the man said, because a salt dome that close to the surface was worth a lot of money. They had one in Avery Island that was hundreds of feet down, but it was still worth millions. He said if Pawpaw could find investors, the Boone family could go into business, drop a shaft, and start selling the stuff. Dan and Lona had gone off to find those investors, but in the meantime, Pawpaw was already selling it, scooping up the rivers of salt that burped out

178

after every rain and bagging it. Hawking it out of his trunk as "Salt of Saint Charles," good for skin troubles, even better for killing bugs and weeds.

Saint Charles was the patron saint of salt and killing things, Pawpaw said in his letter. And never forget that you and Jute started it by digging a pig pen. Imagine! Mr. Abate had filed the papers for a company, and when it had some cash flow he'd get me out of that reform school. I wrote back and said don't waste your money, because I was learning a lot. Though I did miss everybody. I hoped they would furlough me so I could see them, because boys were furloughed on occasion, but they said not to count on it the first year.

In fact, you had to be a saint to get furloughed, didn't matter what year it was, and I was fast going in the opposite direction.

53

Dan

DAN HAD PILED up stones on the rails about three feet high, then dumped armloads of twigs and leaves around it, to start a fire if the stones weren't visible enough. Nobody in his right mind would plow through all those stones, but people who worked on the railroads weren't the best and brightest. They weren't doctors or astronauts for a reason. At least, that's what he told Lona, who was skeptical of the whole idea.

"Wasn't that guy shot?" she asked him.

"What guy?"

"That guy you read about. Didn't the Pinkertons track him down and plug him?"

"Yeah, but he was an editor. Editors don't know nothing."

"You said he got away with it for years. How many trains have you robbed, Dan Boone?"

"Hey, you gotta start somewhere. And we ain't done too good with banks."

"We did *great* with banks. If you hadn't lost all that money, we wouldn't be here at all."

She had a point there, a good one, and that irritated him. He looked down the tracks, which curved up ahead, the roadbed bordered on each side by tall pines. Puffy lava rock covered the bed between the ties, which had supplied the rocks he'd piled up. Lona was now sitting on the pile, her eyes closed in the sun, singing to herself. Minutes passed that way, then Lona asked where the hell it was.

Dan looked at the balky pocket watch he'd glanced at every thirty seconds for the past fifteen minutes. "Should be here already."

"It ain't here."

"I can see that." Dan was sweating in the heat and feeling a bit lightheaded. He stuck the watch in his pocket, got on his knees and put his ear to the burnished surface of the rail, where he heard a soft thrumming of steel on steel. "Won't be long now," he said, hoping he was right. When he stood, he realized he needed to pee, so he unzipped. Lona asked what he was doing.

"I gotta pee."

"You ain't a child. Go in the woods."

"But the train is coming!"

"And what if it does and those rich folks see you peeing? They won't take you serious, a man peeing in the open like four-year-old."

Dan looked down the tracks to where they disappeared. He'd heard something, but still, the train could be miles away for all he knew. He hesitated, cursed to himself, then jogged down the roadbed, through the tall grass of the right-of-way, and into the woods. He was only halfway done when a locomotive came tearing around the bend up ahead.

"Damn it!" he said.

Lona scrambled up and tried to start the pile of leaves with her lighter. But the lighter sparked and fizzled, out of fluid. The train rushed on blindly, with no sign of slowing. Dan was running now, zipping up and shouting. Now a long blast of the locomotive's horn, then another. The earth rumbled as though a vast herd was thundering toward them. Lona faced the onslaught, waving her arms. Dan stopped to work a pistol from his pocket and let off a blast in the air, then another one. Lona shrugged off her red blouse and began flapping it around. Like a bullfighter, Dan thought, like a lady toreador in a lacy bra, the most gorgeous train robber in the world. He was smitten by the sight of her—but not the engineer, apparently, for the train accelerated, its horn snorting in anger. Dan cried for Lona to get the hell off the tracks, it wasn't stopping. But dammit, she didn't hear him with all that noise. The beast rushed on toward its fate—for it would surely crush itself on those rocks, crushing Lona in the process.

"Lona!" Dan cried, but he was drowned out by the noise. "Lona!"

As if in a nightmare, Dan ran up the roadbed, stumbling in the loose ballast rocks, and knocked Lona aside just as the mechanical bull thundered by. An iron stanchion caught her blouse and ripped it from her hand. A great shower of sparks engulfed them as the rock pile was pulverized, and the beast rushed on, bellowing in triumph, Lona's red blouse flapping like a Soviet flag.

Car after car clickity-clacked past, windows filled with faces of soldiers returning home from the Cuban invasion that never was—soldiers who looked in wonder at the two bodies sprawled in the mossy earth that bordered the tracks. Dan and Lona seemed dead to them, sprinkled as they were with grit and dust—like lime thrown on corpses. But once the train was gone, the corpses came back to life and did what men and women naturally do when they've just escaped certain death and one of them is already half naked.

Afterward, Lona found her shoes on the tracks, both of them sliced up by the steel wheels. Which was a great tragedy, to hear her go on about it.

54

THERE WASN'T A FENCE around the reform school, and there was an ice-cream truck that went by every day after class. Boys would run to it and crowd around, especially if the day was hot like it was this day. I didn't have more than a nickel, so I was playing horse on the basketball court. All the boys with money had run off to buy their ice-cream and Eskimo pies and whatever, and when the truck left it turned on the wrong song. Instead of the nursery tune it always played, it played a woman singing "You Are My Sunshine." And the voice was my mother's voice.

I was pretty sure, anyway.

I stood frozen there with the ball. The others said come on, Pig Slopper, shoot the damn ball. Finally I dropped it and took off running after that truck. "Wait up!" I cried. I ran into the road, slowly gaining on it. The driver saw me in his mirror, slowed and pulled over. I had a stitch in my side and could barely speak when I got to his window.

"My mother," I said.

"What you want, kid?"

"My mother...you have my mother."

"What kind of ice cream?"

"It's my mother. She's singing it."

"Hey, you're not one of those idiots, are you?"

"No, no. You're playing that song. My mother's singing it. She's singing it!" He told me to go back to my school and not waste his time. I started running again as he left, staying at his window.

"Get lost. Beat it, will yah?"

"Tell me where she is!" I screamed. "You got to tell me where she is!"

Finally he pushed me and I fell, rolling over and over on the asphalt. A car behind us screeched to a stop. It was a cop car and the cop took me back to the school. Running away from school was the most serious crime of all, and the headmaster made me bend over for what he said was twenty whacks. I was expecting his usual slow swings that did nothing more than send a cool breeze against my legs. But this time was different. He said he'd been keeping an eye on me because I was a devil child. He wound up like a major league pitcher, and with the first swing the paddle split in two and the broken piece flew up and stabbed him in the cheek, right under his eye.

The old Mexican housekeeper saw this and crossed herself. She told him I had *el culo del diablo*—the ass of the devil—and news of this flew around the school. The boys laughed as if this was all a big joke, but the headmaster took it serious. He'd just

185

said he had his eye on me and then he almost lost his eye. The logic, to him, was irrefutable. That one thing led to the other was impossible to ignore—here was a boy with a devil's ass. Such a boy was too dangerous to paddle, so I was never paddled again. This was partly because he retired three months later, and the new headmaster was a softer man, just out of college. He even had a crazy theory that boys shouldn't be beaten or paddled, or otherwise mistreated.

How we marveled at this idea!

The new headmaster pored over the school's extensive records of tortures—leather-bound ledgers resembling the records they kept during the Spanish Inquisition, and he noticed that one boy hadn't been paddled in months. A rising fourth-grader who'd started a Bible group that was well attended by boys who seemed to have become calmer and better adjusted, even if they did spend too much time in the bathroom.

Attention to personal hygiene is not a bad thing, the new headmaster told the monitor who'd brought this to his attention, and later that week he called me into his office.

"Sometimes we only seem to care if a boy lives or dies," he said, scratching his pipe stem thoughtfully against his cheek. "We don't care if he lives a Christian life or not."

"Yes sir, I guess that's right."

"Do you care?"

"About what?"

"About living a life of purity and grace, unpolluted by the base vulgarities of the world?"

"I don't know. I guess I'm like everybody else." I wondered if he knew about my Tijuana Bible, and I was relieved that none of the stories we'd heard had come true. Self pollution wasn't that bad. No one had grown hair on their palms, no one had peed blood, and if there were any cases of insanity, it was hard to tell.

For myself, I'd lost the desire to beat up other boys, and that was both good and bad.

"Most of our boys don't think about higher things," the headmaster went on, "but I don't believe you're one of them. I sense before me a soul as brilliant and unblemished as the sky."

So now I'm a saint, I thought, a perfect little gentleman. This would have ruined my reputation if it had gotten out, but it never got the chance. The next day the headmaster handed me a round-trip bus ticket to Red Church, for a visit just in time for Jute's birthday, paid for by the state of Louisiana. As I was getting on the bus, he slipped me an envelope from Mary Mumford, already opened. He said it was state policy not to deliver mail except from family, but he would make an exception in this case.

I didn't know who Mary Mumford was, but turned out she was our Mary, who'd come home with Uncle Dan that time and pretended to be my mother. She'd sent a letter and two newspaper clippings from the New Orleans paper. She'd written them, too, both of them, probably on that typewriter Mr. Abate gave her. I read every bit of her stories, even the words I didn't understand. The first told how the levee board in Plaquemines parish tried to assassinate her to cover up how they built the levees, which she said were "spoil banks filled with kitchen trash and crawfish heads, no more substantial than marshmallows in a furnace."

That was what she said, every word.

The second was from just a few days before, claiming the president of the Gulf State Bank of Red Church had embezzled half a million dollars and then sparked a panic to cover it up.

He'd paid off the judge and the prosecutor to blame the school principal, Mr. Faat. Tragically, a young boy, who was not guilty of anything (mostly), had been caught up in the affair and sent to reform school.

Mary's letter, in which she called me "my dear Charles," said the judge would probably be arrested and a new judge would set me free. If I wasn't, or if I needed anything, I should write to her in New Orleans.

I folded the letter and stuffed it back in its envelope with the stories. I wondered then if I would ever go back to that reform school. I pressed my face against the window so no one could see the tears. I would really miss that place.

When the bus stopped at the station in Alexandria, halfway to Red Church, I pulled my suitcase down from the rack and looked into the hole I'd made in it. "You doing okay, Zachary Taylor Toad?" I whispered.

The alligator inside just looked back at me with its yellow eye. Alligator Clay hated to give it up, but it was fast getting too big for that watering trough. It was almost too big for my suitcase. I had to leave everything behind to get it in there, but none of my stuff was worth anything anyway. Except the Tijuana Bible, and I gave that to Alligator Clay. I'd told him to keep it safe because it was the secret to my power. And he'd nodded like he did that sort of thing all the time, traded alligators for Bibles.

"Aren't you afraid you'll lose your name?" I'd asked him as I shook his hand.

"Nah, I'll just say I put ole Zak in the swimming hole."

He'd say that too, as that's the way he was. And that'd be the last time anyone went swimming in that swimming hole.

55

MEMAW DROVE ME from the bus station in Red Church with Jute chattering from the backseat. Jute had become a comedian, bombarding me with jokes he'd learned from Bazooka Joe comics, but he still couldn't remember anything but the punch lines.

"And the chicken had chicken teeth!" he said, laughing hysterically because he remembered how funny it was. Then he leaned over the seat and punched my arm. "Get it, Charlie? Get it?"

"Yeah, Jute. That was a good one."

We were still a mile away, yet the parish road already sparkled with salt crystals. I could see Pawpaw's field, bulging ominously over the countryside. When we got to the driveway I saw the sign Pawpaw had put up, announcing his new venture. "Two Spoon Salt Co" flickered overhead in red and yellow neon.

"I don't like it," Memaw said.

"The sign?"

"The two spoons. Like I'll ever get those spoons back."

I slid down in the seat, feeling guilty. Jute hadn't heard her, apparently, because he could hardly contain himself. He opened the door before the car stopped and fell out. Memaw yelled at him, but he didn't pay her any mind. He went running to the house, yelling that Charlie was here, Charlie was here. Like they didn't know I was coming. A new Pontiac was parked next to the house, and a truck I hadn't seen before was parked in the field. Pawpaw came out the house and two men came out the house behind him. I wondered if they were the investors Dan and Lona had gone looking for—those two men with black cowboy hats on their heads and silver guns in their hands.

56

THE MEN WITH THE GUNS invited us inside, even though they didn't live there. Pawpaw didn't like sitting in the living room with all the clouds moving in. He said he needed to get his salt bagged up before it rained. They could have some if they wanted it. Two bags each. It was good for bugs and—

"We're not here for bugs," said a man I assumed was the boss. He was short and had a black mustache that he combed with his finger.

"Then what do you want?" Memaw said.

"Only what your son pilfered from the Great Southern Bank in Baton Rouge. Return our property and we'll be on our way."

"It was criminal what they did," said the other one, who was fat and oily—especially his hair. "That poor boy's never gonna walk again. So unfair." He used a knife to stab a balloon on the wall. Then tried to stab another one but it kept floating to the side. Finally he stuck out his arm like one of the three musketeers and skewered it. He seemed to like stabbing things, so lucky there were plenty of balloons to skewer. Balloons were everywhere, stuck to the walls with tape, or just floating against the ceiling because Pawpaw had filled them with gas from the stove. Cooking gas was lighter than air and a lot cheaper than helium. The balloons were red to celebrate Jute's birthday—red was his favorite color. But they were also there to celebrate my coming home. Along with the fried chicken I could smell from the kitchen, and especially the banner stretched across the wall, with *Welcome home Charlie!* written on it oil paint.

The man with the mustache saw me looking at it and said, "So you're the world-famous Charlie, are you lad?"

"Yes sir, guess I am."

"Where have you been?" He glanced at my suitcase. "Paris? London? New York?"

"Reform school."

He laughed, but the fat one didn't. "Was that in Monroe?"

"Uh-huh."

"I went there."

"Tell me you didn't!" said the mustache man.

"Two years," the fat man said, then turned to me. "They still have that pansy headmaster with his noodle arm?"

"No sir, they replaced him with one out of college."

"Bet he tanned your hide better than Jerome."

"Not really. He doesn't believe in it."

"Doesn't believe in paddling?"

I shook my head.

He frowned like this was a great disappointment.

Jute also was disappointed. "You didn't get whipped, Charlie?"

"Not much," I said.

"Then why'd you go up there?"

"Yeah," said the fat man, "why did you go up there?"

"That ain't none of your business," Memaw said.

"It's my business if I say it is. Hey, why don't you make yourself useful and get me a Dixie?"

"We don't keep any Dixie," she said.

"Then any kind of beer."

"We don't drink."

"Jeez. What kinda hospitality is this?"

"Leave it alone," mustache said, who was now sitting after wiping a chair with his handkerchief. "They said they didn't have any."

"I do have a little moonshine if you want," Pawpaw said.

"You what!" Memaw said, like this was news to her.

"I keep it in the barn. For medical reasons."

"All right then," said the fat man. "Let's go on and get it, and then a big ole plate of fried chicken. That smell is about to kill me."

The mustache man smirked and said, "My Falstaffian friend will eat and drink you out of house and home, and stuff all your worldly goods into that fat belly of his."

Jute whispered to me, "He's gonna eat our house?"

"Clint talks like that," the fat man said, "'cause he reads too many books. But look how little he is! He reads but he don't eat. He's gonna blow away one day, you watch." He patted his Santa stomach and I couldn't help but notice the silver revolver quivering in his pants.

57

JUTE AND ME were sent upstairs with a plate of cake and two jars of red drink even though Jute hated red drink now that it wasn't red anymore because of the government. With Mary gone he had his old room back, and I could smell right away that he hadn't improved it any. The fat man stood at the door and Memaw said for us to eat and go to sleep, and I said no way was I gonna sleep in the middle of the day or lie in pee with those men downstairs.

"Then play with Jute."

"What if they get to, you know?" I looked again at the gun in the fat man's belt.

"They won't get to doing anything. We're just doing some business."

"What kind of business?"

"The kind that's not for children."

"But what if the house burns down?"

"I don't know. Go out the window."

I looked at the window. It was still sunny out, and birds were chirping, but a wall of black clouds was moving our way. "Jute can't go out the window. He's afraid birds will get him."

"I can too," he said, but both me and Memaw could tell he was lying.

"Then hide in the closet."

"No!" Jute said.

"He's afraid the monster lives in there."

"I thought the monster was in the hole?"

Jute nodded.

"He's got monsters everywhere."

Memaw sighed. "I'll leave y'all to figure it out." She closed the door and I heard them going down the stairs.

Jute and me played racecars on the floor, then crazy eights, then go fish after I got tired of telling him the rules of crazy eights. It occurred to me that maybe he couldn't count, but that idea was so pooposterous I quickly forgot it.

Pooposterous was a word I'd learned from Crayon Boy. He was a seventeen-year-old albino who ate crayons to color his poop, a gastro-intestinal art form he'd invented. The world made tons of poop every day, he said, and all of it was pooposterous except his.

Now the wind began to blow and rain pattered against the half-open window. The bedroom door blew open, and I saw all those red balloons coming up the stairs. A huge mass of them collected above the hallway, dislodged by the wind.

"Oh oh," Jute said.

"What?"

"Is that your suitcase over there?"

I looked over at it. "Uh-huh."

"It's moving."

And in fact, it was—I'd completely forgotten about ole Zak. "It's ole Zak," I said. "I have to let him out for a while."

"You got a dog in there?"

"An alligator."

Jute shivered. "Don't let him out. He'll eat me."

"No he won't. He's a tame alligator."

I finally convinced Jute it would be okay, but he sat in the far corner of the room anyway. He had a Dr. Doolittle book in his hand, ready to "bash its lights out" if it came anywhere near him.

Ole Zak was glad to be free, stretching his legs and flicking his tail, and I gave him some of my soda to drink. Jute was amazed that an alligator drank soda, and even more amazed it didn't eat my arm.

"It only eats what people eat," I said.

"Alligators eat dirt."

"Not this one. It's spoiled." I broke off a hunk of cake. "Watch this. It's a trick." I backed over to where Jute was, hiding the cake behind my back. Then I stuck it in the air, saying "Come on, Zak," and Zak ran at me with his mouth snapping, then stood on his hind legs, still snapping. I threw the cake up and Zak caught it, swallowing it whole. This impressed Jute mightily, and he began to howl like he was being murdered.

58

THE FAT MAN ran upstairs to check on us. He had a cigarette in one hand and a chicken leg in the other. "What the hell is going on in here?" he said. He apparently didn't see ole Zak, but ole Zak saw him all right. At least it saw that leg of fried chicken, and ole Zak did his trick, running at the fat man with his mouth snapping and jumping up. The fat man didn't know this was a trick and he stumbled back, colliding with the door. He spun around, screaming, "Get away from me! Get away!"

He still had his cigarette in one hand, the chicken leg in the other, and was stabbing his chicken leg at ole Zak—the worst thing he could possibly have done—then escaped into the hall, flailing. He must have touched one of those balloons with his cigarette, seeing as how it burst into flames, and then they all burst into flames, popping like muffled firecrackers. Fire swirled around and made a nest in the fat man's Brylcreemed hair. Then the flaming hair oil dripped on his clothes so he became one big birthday candle. The wind blowing through the window didn't put it out like you might think. It had gotten dark outside, but inside glowed furiously with the burning fat man. He ran down the stairs screaming, "Whooooo! I'm burning up!"

The banister came loose (as it was missing half its screws) and the fat man slipped and tumbled down. Jute and me went out in the hall and looked after him. The ash of burned-up balloons was raining down and swirling everywhere. The fire was mostly out, and it looked like the fat man was dead. Clint was bent over him, shaking him, saying, "Johnnie, Johnnie, don't die on me."

Jute picked up Mr. Johnnie's gun, which had fallen at the top of the stairs, and Mr. Clint grabbed his own gun and pointed it at us just as Memaw bashed him with a cast iron saucepan, right on his hair. He looked up at her like he was shocked she'd do such a thing. Then she bashed him again and again until Pawpaw wrestled the pan away from her.

Jute and me ran down the stairs. Mr. Clint's eyes were rolled back in his head; he was dead. But when I tried to tell Pawpaw he didn't hear me as he was still wrestling with Memaw and the wind was whooshing in and the windows were rattling. It was a racket worse than the school cafeteria at lunchtime.

59

THE FRONT DOOR SLAMMED open and I tried to close it, but the wind was too strong. Pawpaw had to help me. We ran from room to room, closing windows. Lightning was crashing down. Jute was pointing that gun all around, screaming about monsters, Memaw was yelling to get that fat man out of the house because he was still burning, and Pawpaw was yelling that she'd killed yet another one. She had to stop killing or she'd go to hell. She wasn't going anywhere, she yelled back, and if anybody was going to hell, it was a useless old man who stashed booze in the barn. That hole in the field wasn't anything but a direct highway to perdition, and she expected Pawpaw would be taking it before long.

That was almost the same thing Alligator Clay had said, and I began to wonder if they were right. Especially as the wind really began to blow now, rattling the tin on the roof and howling in the eaves. When the lights went out, Jute began howling too, and Jute and the wind howled together like two wolves.

"Get him to stop that," Memaw said.

"How?"

"Give him some sugar."

"Okay," I said. I twisted the gun from his hand and dragged him by the arm into the kitchen, where Memaw was lighting candles and setting them out in bowls. Shutters were banging outside, and one fell off even as I watched. The sky was as black as Mr. Willis except when lightning blasted the field. Then it was electric blue; yellow sparks flew and showered the ground, burning in spite of the rain.

I got the bag of sugar down from the cabinet and filled up a bowl. Then I sat Jute down and put it in front of him. He wasn't howling anymore, but he was whimpering.

"Spoon," he said.

I got him a spoon and he began eating the sugar, sniffling, licking his lips. "It's good," he said. Memaw came in and said to give him a root beer too. She said if you eat sugar without washing it down, it could go in your lungs and kill you.

"You don't want him to die, do you, Charlie?"

"No ma'am, not till he's old enough."

Memaw had just gone out when the floor shifted and Jute's bowl slid off the table and smashed. He began screaming again, maybe because of the waste of sugar, or maybe because the candles fell off and we were plunged into total darkness. Total darkness was when monsters were happiest, and I'm sure that was exactly what Jute was thinking. So I was almost glad when a flaming bird popped in through the window—passing right through the glass without breaking it—and hovered over the table, fizzing and buzzing with electricity.

I wished Pawpaw could have seen it instead of Memaw, because she came running back into the kitchen with her hair wild, grabbed up the broom and started swinging. The struggle went on for a long time. Crockery broke and pots fell, clattering. Jute and me huddled together under the sink. The bird dodged and danced until it clipped the sink right over our heads and vanished with a gunshot.

Plunged in the dark again, Jute began braying like an angry mule.

Pawpaw came in with a hurricane lamp and wanted to know what the hell we were doing. Memaw stood there wheezing, the broom still in her hands. Then she dropped it, put one hand over her eyes and collapsed in a chair. She moaned that it might've been the Holy Ghost, come to anoint us with grace and save us from destruction, and here she'd beaten it to death with a broom. Pawpaw said most likely it was ball lightning, seeing's how you couldn't kill God with a broom, and she said what did an old boozehound know. She got up and pushed him aside to get her rosary beads from a drawer.

Outside, the hurricane continued to howl.

60

MAYBE IT WASN'T REALLY A HURRICANE, but it rat-
tled the house like one. I went outside about three in the morning when the swirling water was almost up to the porch. Looking
toward the field, I couldn't see anything through the pelting rain.
Still, I got the impression that something was looming out there.
You can sometimes sense a thing even when you can't see it.
Alligator Clay showed me how to do it—you cross your eyes
with your eyelids closed and bend over, trying to look straight
out the seat of your pants. So either you sense something or you
fall over. I did fall over with the wind, and almost slid between
the railings. But I sensed something, I'm pretty sure.

And the next morning I saw what it was—the mountain my
mother had painted on the back of that rice sack. The purest

ghostly white like one of those snow-capped mountains they have on postcards. Right here in the hottest part of Louisiana.

Good thing it hadn't come up under the house, but as it was, the house was tilting to one side. Jute had fallen out of bed in the middle of the night and rolled against a wall. The dead men had rolled too, and were now piled up against the sofa.

Memaw, in the process of cleaning up, dragged them out the door by their boots and dropped them down the steps where the water was now only ankle deep. She said they had overstayed their welcome and she wanted them out. She threw their hats after them, then their guns. Jute went out there and poured a bottle of cough syrup over their heads, for which he got a rare whipping from Memaw. She asked him why he'd wasted good cough medicine and he said because they were sick.

Pawpaw glanced at the bodies when he came back from the field. "Must be fifty feet high," he said, standing next to the fat man, who wasn't so fat anymore since he'd smoldered all night. His face looked bloody with red syrup all over it.

"That's pretty high," I said.

"And three new holes opened up. One's even bigger than Charlie's Hole."

While that was interesting, it was also disappointing. I felt that my hole should always be the biggest.

"Well," Pawpaw said, "I guess we need to get rid of these boys."

"Should we call the sheriff?" I said.

"Oh no. No need to bother the sheriff."

So we did more or less what we'd done before. We got their car and put those men on the backseat, then Pawpaw let me drive it to the water. "Put it in Charlie's Hole?" I asked.

He thought about that, then said I should put it in one of the others so we didn't clog up Charlie's Hole, as he'd sunk a lot of stuff in that one already. "Put it in Jute's Hole."

"Which one is that?"

"On the other side. The biggest one of all."

I confess it irritated me that Jute now had the biggest hole, and he'd never done anything to deserve it except crap all over the field. I drove the car slowly around the mountain and parked it in the salt dunes, right next to the water. This was only the second time I'd driven a vehicle—the first time was at the reform school, and the high school boys said they were very disappointed with me after I ran over a dead porcupine and flattened two tires. But that porcupine shouldn't have been on the road, so it really wasn't my fault.

Pawpaw came around and told me to pop the trunk. He wasn't going to repeat Dan's mistake if he could help it. So I got out and opened it, finding all these shotguns and handcuffs and police tape in there. Pawpaw said they were most likely cops with all that cop stuff. I asked him if we'd made another mistake, and he said yeah, most likely, but there wasn't much to be done about it now.

I put the car in neutral, then we both pushed from the back until the car eased into the water. It floated out to the middle, the seams hissing and bubbling, then it froze up, with the water barely up to the windows.

"Shoot," Pawpaw said, cursing like he almost never did.

"What?"

"It ain't deep enough." He jumped in and waded out to the car. It only came up to his thighs.

About then I heard a car coming, and while I hoped it was Uncle Dan, the crunching was coming from the wrong direction. Pawpaw climbed out and ran a-ways so he could see past the mountain, then he cursed again: "Shoot!"

I ran over next to him and saw the sheriff's car coming up our driveway.

61

"Got a call from the police chief in Alexandria about your boy," the sheriff said, lighting a cigarette with his hands around the match as the wind was still blowing.

"Dan?"

"Uh-huh."

"He's not here," Pawpaw said. "He and Lona are off somewhere."

"That right?" The sheriff flicked the match and looked past us. "Now what the hell is that?"

"What?" Pawpaw said.

"Something's going on around here, that's for sure." He took a few steps so he could see better around the house.

"Nothing's going on."

The sheriff's lips and eyes had gone tight. "That right?"

"Uh-huh."

"Then what am I seeing over there?"

He pointed and Pawpaw didn't look. "Nothing."

"It's nothing," I said, trying to help him out.

"Looks like something to me. Like a mountain of salt."

"Oh yeah," Pawpaw said. "That."

The sheriff looked at him suspiciously. "You forgot you had a mountain of salt in your field?"

Pawpaw scratched his head and seemed at a loss, so I said, "We thought only we could see it. We thought it was a magic mountain."

He looked down at me. "Ah, Charlie. You out of reform school already?"

"Yes sir. For a while."

"And you brought that mountain with you."

"I think the hurricane sucked it outta the ground."

"What hurricane?"

"The one that came through here last night."

The sheriff looked at an uprooted chinaberry tree lying broken in the muddy yard. "Must've been a twister. All I got was some rain."

"Could've been," I said. "All the balloons flew upstairs and caught fire."

"What's that?"

"Nothing, sheriff," Pawpaw said. "Just a dream he had."

The sheriff stared at that mountain now lit up in a beam of light, glittering like a million gems. "You mind if I get a closer look?" he said, and started in that direction even before Pawpaw could come up with some excuse why he couldn't. Pawpaw went after him, yelling at me to get the sheriff a cup of coffee.

IN THE KITCHEN I found Memaw swinging a knife. "No!" I cried and jumped between her and the alligator that was leaping and snapping, trying to eat the butcher knife in her hand. It had cornered her against the refrigerator; fat drops of blood spattered the floor where she'd nicked its nose. "This is just ole Zak," I said. "He's my pet."

"That ain't no pet. That's a goddamn alligator."

"It's just trying to do its trick, that's all."

"It ain't tricking me if that's what it thinks, and it sure ain't staying in the house."

I picked it up and petted the warts on its head. "See, it's not dangerous. And it saved us from those men."

"Uh-huh. How'd it do that?"

So I explained how the fat man burned up thanks to ole Zak, and how he'd be a better watchdog than a real watchdog, and how he only went to the bathroom once a week, and how a swamp boy named Toad entrusted it to me. Memaw softened a bit on account of she knew a family of Toads from New Iberia, but she was still adamant it couldn't stay in the house.

"How about under the house," I said, and she thought about that, finally saying if I put chicken wire up, I could keep it there for a time.

"You'll see what a good watchdog he is," I said.

I locked Zak in the hall closet with a Band-Aid on his nose, and went outside to see about building an alligator house under our house. Jute came flying out and almost knocked me down, wanting to know what that man was doing. That's when I remembered about the coffee, even though I didn't think the sheriff would want any now since he was almost to the top of the mountain. Actually, with some slipping and sliding on all fours, he'd made it to the top and managed to stand there, looking all around. And now he was pointing down the other side, yelling something I couldn't hear. I figured he'd seen the car, and was probably asking Pawpaw what the heck a car was doing floating in that pool of water. Then I blinked and he was gone.

Pawpaw went running around the mountain and me and Jute took off too. I knew that Pawpaw would have a lot of explaining to do if the sheriff found two dead men in the backseat, especially with one of them all burned up and both of them cops. I outraced Jute as usual, and when I turned the corner, I saw the sheriff floating in the water of Jute's Hole and Pawpaw trying to drag him out.

62

WE PULLED the sheriff out and rolled him up on a rusted sheet of roof tin, then tied rope to the tin and dragged it to the house with him on it. After that, Pawpaw took the tractor back to the hole to pull out the car. Memaw came outside and asked what had we done? Had we killed the sheriff?

I was kneeling on the tin next to him and I said, "No ma'am. He's still breathing some."

She came over and pushed me aside. "This ain't good. Your pawpaw is going to jail for sure."

"He just has a knot on his head," I said. "Maybe he won't remember."

She thought about this, then said, "Why don't you get him a soda and some aspirin. He'll probably be feeling it in a minute."

From the porch I saw Pawpaw with the tractor, now dragging that car, leaving great furrows in the salt. I hoped he'd get it in Charlie's Hole before the sheriff woke up.

I knew from television that you hit people on the head if you wanted them to forget. Or else you got them drunk. Better if you did both. So that's why I fixed him a soda half filled from the bottle Pawpaw had in the barn. The sheriff had already hit his own head, so I didn't have to do that part, though I wondered if Memaw might hit him again with that sauce pan for good measure. I was about to ask her when the sheriff began groaning. Memaw knelt next to him to offer him the soda and aspirins.

"What the hell happened?" he said. He was spitting; his whole face was crunchy with salt and looked like he'd swallowed a mouthful.

"You fell," Memaw said, handing him the glass. He grabbed it and the aspirins dropped and slid into the mud. He took a slug and spit it out. "Tastes like gasoline." He wiped his mouth with his wet sleeve and spit again before finishing off the glass in one go. "Jesus. You got any aspirin?"

Memaw sent me back in the house for more aspirin and red drink and I saw the sheriff stand up just as Pawpaw got the car over the levee. The sheriff put his hand up to shade his eyes as the car flipped over, the windshield glinting like a mirror just before slipping in.

"This friggin' stuff," the sheriff said, rubbing his salt-caked eyes. "I can't see a blasted thing. You got a hose pipe anywhere?"

By the time the sheriff drove off, he had a bloody bandage on his head, his eyes were swollen and almost shut, his face cut up, his torn clothes coated with mud and rock salt, his boots squishing with saltwater, and he was staggering from two glasses of moonshine and red drink. Pawpaw and me helped him over to his car. He'd just cranked the engine when he reached over and shut it off again, opened the door and got out.

"What's wrong?" Pawpaw said.

"Damn if I didn't just remember something."

"You did?" Pawpaw said, glancing at me.

"I just remembered why the hell I came out here to begin with."

And he told us what he'd meant to tell us but got sidetracked by our mountain of salt. He meant to tell us that Dan and Lona were wanted after a bank robbery north of Alec. They were on their way out of town in a stolen car when a security device exploded, dying everything like boiled crawfish, and as Dan couldn't see out the windshield worth a shit, he'd swerved off the road and crashed into a utility pole. Wires fell and the car was electrified with two thousand volts for an hour before they could get a crew out there and shut it off.

I felt tears welling up. "Are they dead?" I asked, and he said no, but they probably wished they were. Bank robbery was a pretty serious crime in Louisiana.

"So they're in jail now?" Pawpaw said.

The sheriff scratched salt from his neck. "By rights they should be, but when the electric company finally stopped the electricity and cracked open the car, Dan and Lona were gone."

"They burned up?" I said.

He shook his head. "Not unless they vaporized. There wasn't even a shoelace."

"So how you figure it was them?" Pawpaw wanted to know.

"They left some of their stuff. Like one of those Bibles from the Tijuana Bible Company."

"Lots of people got those," I said.

"You got one, do you?"

"No sir."

"You wouldn't lie to me, now would you, Charlie?"

"No sir, I sure wouldn't." And I didn't, because I'd given it to Alligator Clay.

"Well, that's good. So maybe it wasn't them." He pulled out a cigarette and tried to light it, but the wind kept blowing out his match, and the cigarette was wet, besides. "You know what, I'm kinda feeling lightheaded."

"Maybe you been smoking too much," Pawpaw said.

"Maybe so." The sheriff flicked the cigarette in the mud. "Anyway, best I get on back. I figure if I stay here any longer I might end up dead."

"No sir you wouldn't," I said as he got in. "We wouldn't let that happen."

"Uh-huh." He pulled the car back a little then stopped again, leaned out, dangling something from his hand. "Somebody found this the other day. Don't know if it's your Dan's or not."

Pawpaw took it and looked at it. "I'll ask him when he comes home." He passed it to me—a Timex that had stopped. On the back it said—

To My Devil Dan
Lonalita

"Hey, you find my hat, you let me know?"

"If it didn't blow away," Pawpaw said.

"If it didn't sink in Jute's Hole," I added, and I felt Pawpaw's boot crunching down on my foot.

The sheriff nodded, backed up and then headed down our driveway. He wasn't even weaving too bad.

63

Dan

DAN WASN'T ALL THAT KEEN on camping out, but sometimes you had to do things you didn't like. Or didn't think you'd like, and sometimes you were wrong. Right now he was in a pleasant frame of mind. He was lying in the sun, shirtless, smoking a cigarette and watching Lona as she sat half-naked on the other side of a creek, methodically washing the ink out of twenty dollar bills. Turned out if you washed them before they dried, you could get the ink out. About half of them would be okay, she said, and then she asked him if he was going to help her or what.

"Washing is woman's work," he replied, and that was the last they said for a while. He knew he'd said the wrong thing, but the devil inside him wouldn't let him take it back. He could've explained. He could've said he'd done a year of washing and drying and folding in a prison laundry, and he'd rather have his fingernails pulled out than ever do that again, but he didn't. If she didn't understand him without his having to explain everything, maybe she wasn't the right girl for him. And with that mark on her neck—the mark of Crumb he couldn't help but think—who would have her? A number of names immediately popped into his mind, but he angrily squelched them. Those boys were back in Missouri, and if they even thought they could make time with her, they'd be sorry.

Felonious Crumb, in particular.

He checked his pack of Chesterfields—just three cigarettes left—then looked over where Lona was almost finished. The sun was on her now. Her red hair had turned curly, glistening ringlets pasted to her forehead. A blue dragonfly buzzed between them, then was gone. He went over and sat next to her on a pine log, picked up a twenty, swirled it in the water and draped it on a branch.

"That's a pissant job of washing," she said.

"Best I can do."

She slapped a wet ten on his back, saying it'd dry faster there since he was so fucking hot. Okay, he said, but why was she slapping him so hard? To iron it flat, she said, and then gave him another whack. It stung, but it also felt kind of good; soon the whacking moved on to the next thing, and they slid slowly off the log. The embarrassed faces of presidents floated around them before sinking in the churning water. Not that Dan cared all that much about the waste. There were always more banks, weren't there? The country was full of banks. The government printed money for all those banks day and night, a drowning flood of money that never stopped. So why work for wet pieces of paper? Especially when banks would just give them to you if you asked them right.

At some point while they were rolling around, he asked her to marry him and she said she would if he promised never to look at another woman ever again, and he said yes he'd never look at another naked woman again. *Any* woman, she said, even with their clothes on. And he said yes to that too. But he thought of how they weren't engaged thirty seconds and she was already making demands and he was already lying to her. Which should've made him angry, but it didn't.

"Why are you smiling like that?" she asked.

"Oh," he said, "'cause I'm engaged and it's exactly like I always thought it would be."

"Even lying in a creek?" she asked, and he said yes, even lying in a creek.

64

LIFE WENT ON AT PAWPAW'S HOUSE. I never went back to reform school, and when they sent Pawpaw a letter asking him where I was, he wrote back saying I'd blown away in a hurricane. Okay, they said, but they'd have to see a death certificate, and Pawpaw paid the doctor to send them one. That got me to thinking again that my mother Mary had blown away about as much as I had, so I wrote our other Mary and asked her if she could find out. I got her address from the letter she'd sent me in reform school. She wrote back that she'd look into it. A few weeks later she sent me a Polaroid taken at a cemetery in New Orleans. A Catholic cemetery next to a church. The picture showed a gravestone with plastic flowers bent over in a vase. The stone said:

> Maria Arsenault Holster
> My Only Sunshine
> July 14, 1932–March 3, 1963

I thought at first the sunshine was for me, but then I realized it couldn't be. Whoever had put that on the stone didn't know me at all. Their only sunshine was my mother.

And she'd died while I was in Monroe, slopping pigs.

I called Mary to thank her, and she said maybe the sunshine thing *was* for me. Don't count it out just because it doesn't make sense, she said. Most of life doesn't make sense.

Maybe so. Maybe she was right.

Just a week later my dad Landry Boone tried to escape from Angola and the state police shot him in the back thirteen times. I officially became an orphan that day, or I would have if Pawpaw hadn't got that doctor's certificate saying I was already dead.

Two years later Mousey Bertrand drove a riding mower into Goose Lake and drowned, and I quit school and went to work for the Two Spoon Salt Company. I learned to keep a double set of books and count higher than I ever counted before. We made fifty five thousand three hundred and thirty-eight dollars in a single year selling meat-pickling and nutria-eradicating salt—

With the Holy Ghost in every bag!

—and we told the government we'd made twelve hundred and change. Lying and business went hand in hand, Uncle Dan said.

I never heard from anyone at the reform school except for Crayon Boy. He wrote me from New York where he was doing the same art he did in school. He even had an opening at a SoHo gallery where the crayon company showed up, bought every bit of his artwork, and flushed it. He didn't mind, though. There was a lot more where that came from, he said, and I believed him.

One Saturday Uncle Dan and Lona got married in St. Sebastian's church. The sheriff came in and asked were they running late. Uncle Dan glanced at his new quartz watch and said maybe a little, and the sheriff looked disappointed. Nobody but me asked why they were getting married if they were already married, and all I got for my nosiness was a whack to the back of the head.

I soon got too tall to run under the house, my shoes got too expensive to get them dirty, and even girls didn't seem so stupid anymore. Amy Fontenot got to calling me all the time, and before long I was calling her back, even though I liked her sister better. I became an adult like all the adults in Red Church and kept money in the bank and hoped robbers wouldn't come and clean me out.

People started calling me Mr. Charles instead of Charlie, and I didn't argue with them.

It was a whole lot more fun being a kid, though, what I told Jute one night when he was saying it sucked that he didn't have a car, his own car to go to the A&W and get a soda and a cheeseburger with his friends, and I said did he really want to work to pay insurance and a car note? And he looked at me in this disappointed way, and said he was never growing up and never getting a job, because in his opinion I hadn't been improved by it at all. Not one bit, brother Charles. Not one fucking iota.

I didn't argue with him, of course, as I'd been telling him that all along.

HUB CITY PRESS

HUB CITY PRESS is an independent press in Spartanburg, South Carolina, that publishes well-crafted, high-quality works by new and established authors, with an emphasis on the Southern experience. We are committed to high-caliber novels, short stories, poetry, plays, memoir, and works emphasizing regional culture and history. We are particularly interested in books with a strong sense of place.

Hub City Press is an imprint of the non-profit Hub City Writers Project, founded in 1995 to foster a sense of community through the literary arts. Our metaphor of organization purposely looks backward to the nineteenth century when Spartanburg was known as the "hub city," a place where railroads converged and departed.

Hub City Press *fiction*

New Southern Harmonies • Rosa Shand, Scott Gould, Deno Trakas, George Singleton

Inheritance • Janette Turner Hospital, editor

In Morgan's Shadow • A Hub City Murder Mystery

Comfort & Joy: Nine Stories for Christmas • Kirk Neely

Through the Pale Door • Brian Ray

Expecting Goodness & Other Stories • C. Michael Curtis, editor

TEXT 11/14 Adobe Caslon Pro

DISPLAY Rosewood